Love,
Treachery,

and

Other Terrors

Katharine
Campbell

To Christina
Enjoy!

ISBN: 978-1-09834-492-4 (print)
ISBN: 978-1-09834-493-1 (eBook)

To Sr. Magdalene

Known to me as "Aunt Maura"

Who taught me to love faith, fantasy, and furry things.

1

Fairy Wings (or Lack Thereof)

airies do not have wings. I am not sure why we insist on depicting them that way. Those who have seen fairies describe them as looking like people without any appendages that humans wouldn't normally have. We don't know if this is what they really look like, or if they take human form to put people at ease. We actually know very little about them and they prefer to keep it that way.

What we do know is that they are tasked with helping people learn and practice virtue. Usually, they do this by testing humans. I am sure you've heard stories of fairies taking the form of beggars, blessing those who help them, and cursing those who don't. This is their most common approach, but they have dozens more.

While most fairies are content with this vocation, some deeply resent it. Two in particular come to mind: a mischievous pair of twins by the names of Jace and Acacia. When they were young, they begrudgingly accepted their calling. However, after about a hundred years, they deemed humans predictable and frustrating, persisting in selfishness despite their best efforts.

At last, they started questioning why beings as powerful as themselves should spend their lives in the service of such stupid creatures. They started amusing themselves by manipulating humans. It was much easier to get humans to practice vice than virtue, so they entertained themselves endlessly by tricking

1

people into ruining each other. Jace and Acacia got the same pleasure from toying with the lives of people that children do from crushing fireflies to watch their flattened innards glow.

Fortunately, there is a magical rule that prevents fairies from directly killing humans. And that's a good thing too; otherwise, rebellious fairies would have put an end to humanity long ago. Any fairy that kills a human dies instantly. (I've never seen it happen, but I like to think they explode into sand.) There is one small caveat: a fairy can kill a human, if the human attacks first.

This rule was not much of a hindrance to Jace and Acacia because they were exceptionally good at getting humans to kill each other. Their intelligence was far superior; they had magic beyond measure and a complete disregard for the lives of others.

After Jace and Acacia had caused three wars, the Fairy High Council sentenced them to two millennia in prison. The only way to contain a fairy is to seal it in a magic bottle. These are the same magic bottles used to contain genies. (You can actually use them to contain anything; they are very handy that way.)

So they were imprisoned and their bottles hidden away in a desert cave. The Fairy High Council filled the cavern with snakes and scorpions, and left feeling confident that the bottles would remain undisturbed by curious mortals.

They really should have known better.

2

Fausta's Treason

Princess Fausta was a curious mortal who happened to be in desperate need of a genie. She was having some family problems. They were the type of problems she figured only magic could resolve. While finding a genie was no easy task, Fausta was relentless in her search and persisted for many months seeking clues and following rumors.

Her persistence was rewarded. She found the desert cave and ordered her attendants to burn out the inside. She knew that fire could neither destroy a magic bottle nor the creature it contained. The vipers that guarded the cave, however, were quite a different matter. When the air within the cavern cleared, and it was safe for Fausta to enter, she found herself stepping over piles of charred snake bones. She wasn't squeamish and might even have stopped to examine the fragmented skeletons if it wasn't for the urgency of her task.

Her high head and strong features gave her an aura that demanded respect. Like most Kalatheans, she had olive skin and thick black hair. Hers tumbled over her shoulders in waves and curls. Her dark eyes held keenness and a resolve; she was the type of person who couldn't be dissuaded once she set her mind on something.

Though her personal guards objected, she insisted on entering the cave alone. She did not want to risk anyone else claiming her prize. When she spotted the two bottles nestled in a rocky alcove, she was overcome with delight. Could she really be lucky enough to find two genies?

She took the first bottle, pulled a corkscrew from her pocket, and removed the seal. It flew off with a loud POP and a blinding flash. Smoke filled the cavern and there stood Acacia blinking and fanning the air with her hand.

She was a beautiful, imposing figure—perhaps the only person who could intimidate the haughty princess before her. She stood only slightly taller than Fausta, but she had a regal air about her, and it gave her the illusion of greater height. Her skin was white and her hair was the deepest black Fausta had ever seen. She should have been beautiful, but there was something unnatural about her appearance, which made Fausta feel uneasy.

"Has it been two thousand years already?" Acacia asked groggily. Then, she noticed the princess. "Who are you?"

Fausta spoke boldly as if unfazed by the presence of the otherworldly being.

"I am Princess Fausta of Kalathea," she replied, pulling the cork from the second bottle. It came loose immediately without a pop, but smoke still filled the room. When it cleared, Jace was standing beside his sister.

Jace would have been a perfect replica of his sister, if he wasn't male. He had the same white skin and the same dark hair (though his was cut short). Fausta thought he was more beautiful than a man ought to be.

"Jace," Acacia smiled. "How long were we imprisoned?" The grogginess had left Acacia almost instantly and she looked fresh and bright, the way irritating morning people do the moment they roll out of bed.

Jace, however, still needed a moment to recover himself.

"I don't know." He looked around the cave taking everything in. "I thought it had only been a thousand years. Not that I'm complaining, but why'd they let us out?"

"*They* didn't," Acacia answered cheerily. "This sweet lady saved us. Isn't that nice, Jace?"

"Oh," Jace replied, regarding the princess. "Yes, how very kind of her."

"Perhaps we should do something to thank her for setting us free?" Acacia suggested.

A smirk flickered across Jace's face. "Absolutely!"

Acacia addressed the princess: "Tell me, what reward can we give you? What would make the fleeting decades of your life more pleasant?"

"I was hoping for three wishes," the princess answered.

"Three?" laughed Jace. "She's a bold one isn't she? She only rescued us once."

"Now, Jace," his sister reasoned. "There are two of us, so that's two wishes at least."

Fausta knelt before them. "I do not wish to try your patience," she answered. "A single wish is all I require."

"Then why did you ask for three?" Jace grumbled.

"Well, just because, I thought three was standard for genies."

"GENIES!" Jace cried. "You think we—"

But Acacia held up her hand to silence him.

"Only in legends, my dear," she answered. "We can give you as many, or as few as we deem appropriate. Tell us what it is you desire."

Jace glared at his sister and mouthed: *I hate genies!*

She mouthed back: *I know. Shut up.*

Fausta's face was bent toward the ground in reverence, so she did not notice the exchange.

"My father, King Basil the Fourteenth, recently expired."

"Just like old cheese," Jace mumbled. Acacia shot him a glare.

"I have two brothers. An elder brother by the name of Justin—a warrior in the prime of life. My younger brother's name is Alexander, a boy of sixteen. It was always assumed that Justin would inherit the throne, but upon my father's deathbed, he named *Alexander* heir."

"How interesting," Acacia answered. "Did he say why?"

"It was something about Justin and I being evil; I wasn't sure what he was saying because he was dying at the time," Fausta replied.

5

Jace picked up his bottle and tapped the opening into his palm. A long stick slid out, far longer than the length of the actual bottle. The end of it was burned into charcoal. Jace took it and started noting the names of Fausta's father and brothers on the wall.

He paused, rubbed his hand along the wall, and observed the soot that stuck to his fingers.

"Did you light our cave on fire?" he asked.

"There were sn—"

"No matter," he interrupted with a wave of his hand. "Continue."

Fausta noticed the ash on the wall where he was writing disappear, leaving only the words Jace had written:

Justin, Fausta, Alexander.

"So what is your wish?" Jace asked.

"I wish to be queen," Fausta petitioned. "In Alexander's place."

"That's cheating," Jace commented.

Fausta looked confused.

"That's a hundred wishes in one," he clarified. "You are asking for power, respect, riches, a title, and the removal of your brothers."

Fausta opened her mouth to answer, but Acacia cut her off.

"It may be beyond your power, Jace," she smirked. "But it certainly isn't beyond mine."

"I never said it was beyond me," Jace objected. "I am only saying that the princess can't count."

Acacia smiled sweetly at Fausta. "Do you really want to be queen?"

"More than anything," Fausta answered.

"Then you shall be," Acacia confirmed.

The dark cave suddenly became bright as day though Fausta could not find the source of the light.

"That's better," Acacia observed. "Blow out your lamp, my dear. Save the oil. Let's begin planning."

"Planning?" Fausta asked. "Can't you just... snap your fingers or something?"

"Perhaps that's how it works in stories," Jace answered. "But in the real world, magic is much more complicated. We will need your complete cooperation."

"That's right," Acacia added. "You'll need to answer our every question honestly if this is to work."

"Don't lie to us," Jace warned. "If you lie to us, we'll know. We know everything!"

"But if you know everything, then why do you need to ask—" Fausta began saying.

"First," Acacia interjected. "What does your husband think of all this?"

"I don't have a husband."

Jace scrutinized her. "How old are you?"

"Twenty-six, what does that have to—" Fausta was saying.

"A princess? Twenty-six and unmarried?" he questioned. "How unusual."

"I've been married," Fausta answered. "Three times."

"Three times!" The fairies exclaimed in unison.

Fausta nodded then sighed deeply. "They all died."

"I am so sorry," Acacia replied softly. "How?"

"I blame myself really," Fausta recalled. "The first was carrying me off after our wedding celebration, when he tripped and landed on my knife. The second died during our wedding feast when I accidentally spilled hemlock juice in his drink, and the third died of a heart attack after our vows. I don't blame myself for that one; he was a very old man. It was just luck, I suppose."

She stared wistfully into the distance and then added, "Bad luck. Very, bad, luck!"

She pulled a handkerchief from her pocket and dabbed her nose. "With three husbands dead, my father couldn't find me another suitor. So here I am, doomed to shape my fate as I see fit."

"How unfortunate for you," Jace sighed. "Three dead husbands, a dead father, two dead brothers…"

"My brothers aren't dead," Fausta corrected.

"But they will be!" Jace answered cheerily. "When you kill them!"

"Who said anything about killing my brothers?" Fausta asked.

"Um, you did," Jace replied. "When you wished for the throne."

"But—" Fausta began.

"It's all part of the magic," Acacia explained. "Do you want this kingdom or not?"

"More than anything," Fausta insisted.

"Then you have to do what we tell you, my dear."

Acacia took the charcoal from Jace and found a flat spot on the cave wall. First, she drew Alexander. She had no idea what Alexander looked like, so she just imagined Fausta as a sixteen year old boy.

"It's his perfect likeness," the princess marveled.

Acacia then drew Justin beside the young king, imagining how the princess would look as a man in the prime of life. She stepped back for a moment scrutinizing her work and then tapped the charcoal on his face to add stubble.

"How do you draw so well?" Fausta asked.

"Magic, of course," Acacia explained, though in truth, it was from a thousand years of practicing on the inside of her bottle. "The plan is simple. First we must plant rumors among the Kalatheans to build hatred and distrust toward the young king Alexander. At the same time, we must spread word of Justin's charity and kindness."

"That is going to be difficult," Fausta replied. "Justin is a violent drunk. He's currently away pillaging neighboring kingdoms."

Acacia rolled her eyes. "No matter, Justin's character will only be a minor hindrance. We'll alter his image then proceed to the fun part."

"What's the fun part?" Fausta asked.

"When Justin returns from the war, you stab him in the back!"

"Figuratively?" Fausta questioned.

"And literally!" Acacia clarified.

Fausta gave a little shrug and a nod. "Alright, and then what?"

"Then find Alexander and cry: 'brother, brother, something terrible has happened!' When he says: 'what is it, my dear sister?' you say, 'I'll show you!' Then, you take him to Justin's corpse and while he is still gaping in horror you—"

"STAB HIM IN THE BACK!" Jace interjected. He was too excited to contain himself.

Acacia sent Jace an annoyed glare. "Then throw yourself over Justin's body, weeping and wailing and calling for the guards! When they enter, tell them you saw Alexander murder Justin and you were filled with a holy vengeance and killed him."

Fausta furrowed her brow, thinking through the whole thing carefully.

"In this way, you will rule the hearts of the people," Acacia concluded. "They will uphold you as a beloved hero for avenging their dear prince and when you lay claim to the throne, they will support you."

Fausta was quiet for a long moment.

"Is something troubling you, princess?" Acacia asked.

"Do we really need to kill Alex?" she asked. "Why not just banish him, or throw him into prison or something?"

Jace and Acacia both regarded her for a moment and then exchanged a look.

"Is there some reason you wish to keep him alive?" Acacia asked.

"Well, I don't know," the princess shrugged. "He's a child. He's not like Justin. He's not cruel or greedy…."

"So what is he?" Jace inquired.

"He's, well, he's sixteen," Fausta continued. "Mostly he just reads and eats. Sometimes he mumbles. He's been so lost since he was crowned. He wanders the palace with the anxious stare of a newborn calf. He's been coming to me for advice constantly."

Fausta rubbed her forehead.

Acacia looked at the princess with soft eyes full of compassion. "You really are the only person keeping the kingdom together, aren't you?"

The princess responded with a deep sigh. "If only you knew."

"Your people need you, princess," Jace observed. "Where would Kalathea be without you?"

"A wasteland of poverty and sickness," Acacia finished. "You know something? I think you will be remembered as one of history's most powerful women. Little girls for generations to come will admire you. Because of your reign, the world will come to realize that women can do anything men can. You have no idea how important it is that your wish comes true."

"But Alex hardly deserves to die," the princess remarked.

"Your hesitation is understandable," Acacia said. "But if you imprison Alexander, the people will perceive you as soft."

"And you cannot appear soft to anyone," Jace asserted. "Your enemies will see your sex alone as a sign of weakness. 'Kalathea has a woman on the throne,' they will say. 'She's gentle,' they will say. 'Let's sack Kalathea,' they will say. You must prove that you are as ruthless as any man and avenging Justin is an excellent way to start."

"I've never killed anyone who didn't derserv—" Fausta started. "I mean, Alexander's not like other men. He's very gentle. He's...*weak*." She paused, unsure if *weak* was the right word. She couldn't think of a better one so she continued. "While Justin is off splitting skulls, Alexander is home asking how this edict or that law will affect the common folk. It's very sweet but entirely impractical."

"His gentleness is a product of naivety," Acacia answered. "In time, he'll be like every other man: self-absorbed and cruel."

"All men?" Jace objected, shooting his sister a look.

Acacia glared at him. "Especially you."

"It's true," Jace admitted with a smirk.

"What will it be, princess?" Acacia asked. "Will you save your country?"

Fausta was silent.

"You admire Alexander's concern for the people," Jace added. "But you don't seem concerned for them yourself. How will they fare under the reign of an unfit king?"

"Alright," Fausta agreed, though her tone seemed uncertain. "I'll do whatever it takes."

"Excellent!" Acacia replied. "I have a simple formula that will serve us well." She started writing on the wall.

"Formula?" Fausta puzzled.

"Yes, my dear; there's a science to tainting a person's reputation. Now tell me, where do people talk?"

"I don't understand," the princess answered. "People talk everywhere."

"Of course," answered Acacia. "But people talk more in some places than others. For example, do you have a marketplace? Pubs? Churches?"

"Oh!" Jace was giddy with excitement. "Gossip flourishes in church congregations!"

"I really don't under—" Fausta began.

"Hush!" Acacia interjected. "Just listen, my dear! You will begin in your home. I am sure Alexander is the topic of much conversation at the palace. Jace and I will begin with the common folk. Start a conversation with anyone you can, and begin by mentioning one of Alexander's good qualities."

"Good qualities?" Fausta questioned. "Aren't we trying to destroy him?"

"Yes," Acacia replied. "But you don't want people thinking you're a gossip!"

"Wait, but… aren't we?" Fausta asked.

Acacia continued ignoring Fausta's question. "It also makes them more likely to believe you when you say less than complimentary things. That brings me to my first equation."

She started writing on the wall with her charcoal, then stepped back to reveal the following:

(Good quality) + *"But, I'm concerned"* + *(Legitimate concern)* = *doubt.*

"For example," Acacia explained. "You could say: 'Our king seems like a kind person, doesn't he? But I'm concerned because he's so young! Do you really think he'll be a capable ruler?'"

"I don't see how that helps us," the princess commented. "There is nothing false in that and it seems like something that should be discussed."

Acacia smiled. "It's not the sentence itself that's damaging, but rather who discusses it and how they discuss it. You see, if the young king's advisors discussed this concern, they would be able to provide him help and guidance that would make him a stronger king. We don't want him to be a stronger king; we want him to be a dead king. So we need to be sure that the people who discuss these concerns are the people who can't do anything to address them. Then, we can move on to the next portion of the plan."

She wrote a second equation below the first:

(Doubt + potential consequences of legitimate concern) × the human imagination = fear.

"There are many potential consequences of the king's inexperience. Why don't you name a few?" Acacia asked.

"I've got one!" Jace interjected. "He may not fully understand the grave responsibilities he has to his people! He might neglect his duties and use his wealth and position for his own amusement."

"Yes!" Acacia answered. "And once that fear is planted, we draw attention to everything young Alexander does that isn't directly related to his kingly duties. What else? Surely our princess has some ideas?"

Fausta thought. "Well, I suppose our enemies could see his age as a sign of weakness and launch an attack."

"Marvelous!" Acacia said. "Speak of these potential consequences to anyone and everyone, and if you have any evidence at all that they might come to be, draw attention to it, exaggerate it! Then, we can begin the final part of the plan."

Acacia began writing again and as she wrote she explained: "Anger is a natural reaction to perceived injustice. Once the people are afraid, they will be watching for injustices in everything Alexander does. You should watch the young king too. Every time he misspeaks, make it known to as many as possible.

Read meaning into everything he says and does and spread your conclusions to every waiting ear."

She stepped away from the wall; now it read:

Fear + the perception of injustice = hatred

"Once the people are sufficiently angry, you can say anything about the king, true or false, and people will believe you without question. Only when the people hate him can you kill him. You see, he'll already be dead in their hearts. Killing him will be a formality," Acacia added.

The princess was looking at the stone floor, lost in thought.

"How long will all this take?" she asked.

"Has the Internet been invented yet?" asked Jace.

"I take it from the princess's perplexed expression that the answer is no," Acacia said and cracked her knuckles. "We'll just have to go about this the usual way. When is Justin coming back?"

"When the war season ends," Fausta answered.

"That will be plenty of time," Acacia replied.

They then went on to discuss ways of building up Justin's reputation. According to Acacia, it could be done by crediting him with acts of charity, distributing goods to the people in his name, and dismissing any of the servants who actually knew him personally.

Fausta suggested that it might be easier to paint Alexander as the beloved victim and Justin as the cruel killer, but Acacia was intent on keeping the original plan.

Jace and Acacia returned with Fausta to Lysandria, the Kalathean capital. Jace lived as a merchant in the city where he worked tirelessly to poison the king's good name. Acacia became one of Fausta's handmaidens and worked with her to spread distrust in the palace.

The more time Fausta spent in Acacia's company, the more Acacia manipulated her desire for power and her resentment toward Justin. As the time to execute their plan approached, Fausta did not have second thoughts about killing him.

It was Alexander she had second thoughts about killing. Second thoughts and third thoughts, and finally when the moment came and Alexander stood with his back to her, gaping at the sight of Justin's corpse, she couldn't bring herself to do it.

Acacia had concealed herself from human view by magic and stood in the room watching the princess to see if she would follow through. When she saw her hesitation, she immediately revealed herself and started screaming for the palace guards.

They poured in to see Acacia, Fausta, and Alexander standing by the body of the prince. Acacia's expression was anguished, tears streamed down her cheeks. Fausta was white-faced and trembling head to foot. Alexander had been frozen since the moment he noticed his lifeless elder brother.

With the guard, came everyone else who was within the sound of Acacia's cries: servants, nobles, and palace guests. Most looked in sorrow upon their beloved prince. Some (the few remaining who knew him in life) thanked God silently and excused themselves.

Jace entered with the crowd and was the first of them to speak.

"What happened, princess?" he asked. "Who is responsible for this heinous crime?"

Fausta had a choice to make.

The people hated their king so much that a word from her would condemn him. No one would question her. However, when she saw the confusion in her little brother's face, she found herself unable to speak. Her lust for power battled with her affection for him.

As a princess, Fausta was used to getting her way (except in a few small things like marriage and career choice). Most of the time, if she wanted something, she got it. At the moment, she wanted to take over the kingdom without killing her little brother.

She had an idea.

"When I heard that the prince had returned I came down to greet him," she recalled. "But when I entered… I saw…" She looked at Alexander with a betrayed expression. Alexander looked back, eagerly awaiting her testimony.

"I saw the king driving a knife into his back."

There were so many holes in this story that you could use it as a colander, but the people didn't care. They'd been waiting for an excuse to kill Alexander for so long they swallowed it without question.

Alexander would have been torn apart right then and there, had the guard not intervened. As they held the rabble back, they looked to Fausta for instructions. She ordered them to arrest Alexander, which they did immediately. Any loyalty they had to the young king was dissolved by the toxic murmurs of the people long ago.

It was clear to every person present that true power resided with the princess. The Kalathean Senate was quick to confirm that no law existed prohibiting a woman from ruling. They went on to attribute the late king's choice of heir to madness brought about by his illness. So it was that Fausta was named queen within a few hours of Justin's murder.

Her first act was to sentence Alexander to death. Though her enthusiastic subjects wanted to carry out the sentence immediately, she insisted it be done at dawn.

"Dawn is standard for executions. What kind of a queen would I be if I violated Kalathean traditions on a whim?"

The next morning, when the guards came to fetch Alexander, they found his cell empty. The city and all surrounding villages were searched to no avail. When the guards brought the queen the news of the futile hunt, she ordered the matter dropped.

3

As Alexander Saw It

Alexander sat at a table in the palace library. He was staring at the open pages of a book titled: *The History of Kalathean Tax Law*. Despite the exhilarating nature of the text, he couldn't focus.

His features resembled those of his sister, but his demeanor made it clear he lacked her confidence. His large brown eyes gave him a naturally anxious look. Since he was always worried about something, it suited him. In that moment, the subject of his concern was alternatively the memory that kept disrupting his focus, and the fact that his focus kept being disrupted.

Every time he caught his mind wandering, he scolded himself. Then, he would think about how undisciplined he was, and how dangerous it was for a king to be undisciplined, and how his father never should have made him king in the first place; then he would remember the awful evening his father named him heir, and the book would remain unread.

He remembered that moment—he was racing through the palace halls crying out to everyone within earshot: "Find the doctor!"

He could still hear his father calling from his chamber. "Alexander! Come back here at once!"

The doctor, a stick of a man in a deep blue robe, suddenly appeared at the end of the hall and hastened toward him. The man didn't run, rather, he walked in long strides that were equally efficient. Alexander felt a flicker of relief.

"What's happened, Your Highness?" the physician asked with a bow.

"I think my father has developed a fever; he's delirious," Alexander replied.

The doctor followed him back to the king's chamber. It was a vast room, separated from a broad balcony only by a long silk curtain. In the bed, in the center of the room, lay King Basil the Fourteenth, or what was left of him.

The once magnanimous ruler was a frail shell of a man. He was propped up on a pile of pillows looking at Alexander with a slightly irritated expression.

"I'm not delirious," he stated.

"He doesn't seem delirious," the physician agreed.

"Check, please!" Alexander urged. "He just said the strangest thing."

"What did he say?" the doctor asked.

"That I am making Prince Alexander my successor," Basil replied. "I've never made a more sound-minded decision."

"Wait a moment," the physician questioned. "Are you saying Justin is no longer the crown prince?"

"That's exactly what I'm saying," Basil asserted.

"Praise God!" the physician exclaimed. Then turning back to Alexander he added, "No, he's not delirious."

"Thank you, doctor," the king said. "You may go." He pointed a bony finger toward Alexander. "*You* stay."

The physician left with a cheery smile.

Alexander remained petrified. His apprehension made evident by eyes a size larger than normal. He had a habit of fiddling with whatever he was holding when he was nervous. Since he wasn't holding anything at the moment, he took a bit of his sleeve and rolled it between his thumb and forefinger. "But, but, Justin…" he stammered.

"Is a drunk," Basil stated, "a cruel and violent drunk who would bring ruin upon this kingdom."

Alexander's mouth fell open. In his sixteen years of life, he had never seen his father diverge from his usual method of dealing with Justin's behavior—ignore it until Justin made a scene and embarrassed the family. Then send Justin on a pilgrimage to do penance, assume him cured, and never discuss the matter again.

"Your sister was right about him," the old king sighed. "And I cannot bear to face God having left my people in a tyrant's care."

"I wouldn't be any better," Alexander defended. "Besides, you won't have to face God for a long time."

The king's expression softened. He motioned for Alexander to take a seat in a chair by the bed. Alexander obeyed.

"I am not going to recover," Basil said.

"Of course you will," Alexander objected. "I've prayed for a miracle unceasingly, and I have faith that God will save you."

The king smiled faintly. "It is so easy for you to believe that God can save me, yet so difficult for you to believe that God can make you a great king."

Alexander wrung his hands. "That has nothing to do with God. It is my own weakness that makes me unsuitable."

"And your failures are stronger than God's grace?"

"That's not what I said," Alexander mumbled.

"That's precisely what you said," Basil retorted. "If making excuses paid, you'd be richer than Solomon. Stop doubting and accept your responsibility."

"Justin is going to kill me," Alexander breathed. He actually meant it. Few things terrified him more than his brother.

"How?" Basil replied. "You control the palace guard and the army."

"Right," he mumbled.

His father had made it sound so simple. Certainly, he had all the resources of Kalathea at his disposal, but even as he sat in the library trying to focus on his book, he was dreading Justin's return.

The sound of footsteps in the hallway jerked him fully out of his memory. He was alone in the room, reading by candle light, twirling one of his dark curls with his forefinger. He could feel himself trembling as the person approached. He breathed a sigh of relief when he saw it was only Fausta.

He was safe for the moment. He scolded himself again for letting his mind wander and looked back down at his book. His father had been dead for weeks now, yet seemed more present than ever.

He wasn't honoring his father by letting his memories distract him. He was truly the worst king in Kalathea's history. Well, except maybe for Justin the Incinerator who was something of an arsonist, but at least he—

"Alex," came Fausta's voice.

Alexander jumped. She was now standing right in front of him. Up close, she looked completely distraught which was alarming because he had never seen her distressed about anything (even the deaths of her three husbands hadn't shaken her). Her face was white, her hands were trembling, and her brown eyes were wide with horror.

"Alexander," she breathed. "Something terrible has happened."

"Shall I call the guards?" Alexander asked.

Fausta shook her head. "Just come quickly."

Alexander didn't hesitate. As he stood, he instinctively felt for his knife. He usually wore it on his belt, but misplaced it earlier that day. Fausta had her dagger, which was a slight relief. She kept a hand on it as they walked and fiddled with the hilt nervously.

The halls were quiet as they usually were in the evening. They passed only the occasional servant, but Fausta urged him not to speak to anyone. He felt his heart pounding.

What possibly could have happened to make Fausta behave this way? Now and then, he felt her looking at him, but when he turned to meet her eyes, she looked away.

He glanced down at her hand, observing how she rolled her fingers up and down the hilt of her weapon. It was only then that he noticed the scarlet droplets staining her sleeve.

"Are you hurt?" he whispered.

She glanced at him for a brief second and just shook her head. But she was hurt, she had to be. How else would she get blood on her clothes? Unless someone else was wounded and she was helping that person. But then, why wouldn't she send for a doctor? And why didn't she want him talking to anyone?

"Fausta, if you are hurt we should—"

"I'm not hurt, Alex," she hissed. "Keep quiet. You're making this… ugh… just keep quiet."

Now, he was thoroughly perplexed. Not knowing what else to do, he followed quietly until they came to a secluded room in the very back of the palace. It was a large storage room, full of jars and dried goods.

That's where Alexander found his missing knife. It was lodged in Justin's back. He gaped at the horrid sight. For a few moments, he was completely paralyzed. Then, he looked back over his shoulder at his sister. She was paralyzed also—standing with her dagger in her raised hand.

Seeing his sister standing before him, with her blade frozen mid-strike made Alexander realize something. Justin's murderer must have been standing right behind him. He twirled around but saw no one. He looked back at his sister; she had lowered her blade and was rubbing her forehead with one hand.

"Oh, Alex," she sighed. "Why do you have to… be you?"

Alexander had no idea what she was talking about. He was too shocked to think much of anything at the moment, except that he should probably call the guards before his brother's assassin escaped. He opened his mouth but couldn't speak.

Then, someone shrieked, and the next thing he knew, people were pouring into the room. They gasped at the awful sight.

"What happened, princess?" someone cried. "Who is responsible for this heinous crime?"

For a small eternity, the whole room seemed to hold its breath. Fausta looked at Alexander, then toward the spectators, and then back at him.

"When I heard that the prince had returned I came down to greet him," she recalled. She was obviously terrified. Alexander had a horrible thought. What if Justin attacked her? Maybe she accidentally killed him while trying to get away… by stabbing him in the back… with Alexander's knife. Nothing about this made sense.

"But when I entered… I saw…" she looked at Alexander with a betrayed expression. Alexander looked back, eagerly awaiting her testimony. She had to know he would never punish her for defending herself.

"I saw the king driving a knife into his back," Fausta finished.

Though most of the evening was a confused blur in Alexander's mind, he remembered those words with perfect clarity.

The next thing he knew, he was face down on the stone floor shielding the back of his head with his hands as the crowd swarmed over him. The guards intervened, pushing back the rabble. They helped him to his feet only to bind his hands.

His head throbbed. He could feel blood trickling down from his temple. Everyone was shouting. As the guards led him away, he looked backward over his shoulder and spotted Fausta, standing among the people, staring at the floor despondently.

"Fausta!" he called.

She glanced up at him briefly, then back down at her feet.

4

Escaping Death and Other Surprises

Alexander would have been happy to give up the crown if it didn't also mean losing his head. He paced back and forth across his tiny prison cell, rebuking himself for not being more vigilant. His father tried to warn him that something like this might happen. In the weeks leading up to his death, the king would say things like, "be careful who you trust, son," and "even those closest to you could turn on you, son," and "Fausta is definitely going to try to murder you and take over the kingdom, son."

Alexander paid little heed to this warning. He couldn't imagine Fausta doing something like that and, without his father, who else could he turn to for advice?

Growing up, it was Fausta who defended him from Justin's cruelty, and it was Fausta who came up with clever and subtle ways to exact vengeance on their brother. When Alexander was very little, he'd trail after Fausta all day with wide eyes full of admiration. Even when they had grown, he still looked at her like that from time to time. She always knew what needed to be said and could find a clever way out of any situation, no matter how difficult.

After his father named him heir, he begged him to consider giving the honor to Fausta. His father refused.

"Why?" Alexander asked. "She is just as capable as any man."

"And as ruthless," his father added.

"She's never been anything but kind to me," Alexander insisted.

"You've never been a threat to her," his father replied.

Alexander hugged himself with his arms. The prison was cold and he'd been stripped of his long kingly tunica and dressed in a worn linen garment. It was sleeveless and only came to his knees.

It occurred to Alexander that he'd be seeing his father again in the morning. He'd probably have to spend the first few hours of eternity listening to a long lecture about how he shouldn't have let his guard down.

He could just imagine the exchange. His father would say: "Alexander, what are you doing here so soon? You didn't let Justin kill you, did you?"

Then, Alexander would say: "Um, it wasn't Justin. I may not have fully heeded your warning about Fausta."

Then his father would sigh deeply and give him that awful look. That look so full of disappointment—it made Alexander wish that the Earth would swallow him up.

He played out several variations of the lecture that was to follow in his mind, until he was almost on the brink of insanity. In that moment, neither Fausta nor all the people of Kalathea hated Alexander more than he hated himself.

Alexander wanted nothing more than to honor his father by being the best king he could be. Unfortunately, there was more to being a good king than what he could learn from books. Kings always knew what to say. Alexander never knew what to say. Kings knew how to build relationships. Alexander was terrified of people. Kings were eloquent. Alexander's every sentence was punctuated by "ums" and "uhs." He could understand but not express his understanding. When he spoke, he made a fool of himself.

His father originally planned to send him off to a monastery when he came of age. He did not understand why his father changed his mind. Alexander longed for what could have been. A life of quiet contemplation and icon painting. What did it matter now? In the morning, he'd go to his father a failure, and that bothered him more than anything.

His head throbbed. Instinctively, he tried to rub the gash above his eyebrow, but winced when his fingers brushed it.

He lay down on the stone floor and curled himself into a tight ball. He struggled to keep his eyes open. Sleeping would only bring the dawn faster. Even if they were miserable, he wanted to experience the last few hours of his life. His weariness soon overcame him and neither pain, nor cold, nor a fretful mind could keep him from falling asleep.

He was startled awake by the sound of footsteps and the warm glow of lamplight. Assuming it was the guard coming to get him, he rose to his knees, folded his hands and prayed that God would forgive him for being a terrible king, and a terrible son, and a terrible person all around.

"*Alex*," came a harsh whisper.

"Fausta?" he replied, opening his eyes. Sure enough it was his sister who stood before him with a lamp in one hand and the guard's key ring in the other. She was glancing around nervously.

He felt a rage bubbling up inside him. There were so many things he wanted to say, but he couldn't find the words to express them. So instead, he turned his back to her and stood with his arms crossed, glaring at the floor.

"Alex, you need to come quickly," Fausta ordered. "If you aren't out of here by dawn, they'll kill you."

Alexander looked over his shoulder at her with one eyebrow raised. "Wasn't that the idea?"

"Oh, Alex," she replied. "You didn't think I was actually going to have you killed, did you?"

Alexander was too confused to think anything. All he could do in that moment was feel a strange combination of rage, anxiety, and suddenly, a tiny glimmer of hope.

"I'd never kill you, little brother," Fausta assured. "Not if I could avoid it."

Alexander had no idea how to reply. He just stared at her with an expression of disbelief and then obediently followed her. The guards who usually patrolled the halls were strangely absent. He couldn't help but wonder what Fausta had done to get rid of them. When they finally emerged from the prison, he could see that it was still the dead of night. They didn't see another soul as they slipped through the sleeping city, weaving their way through the backstreets.

Lysandria was beautiful. The buildings were decorated with pillars and mosaics and there was at least one fountain in every square. Alexander couldn't believe how desperate he was to escape it.

When they drew near the main gate, Fausta gave him her necklace and instructed him to sell it in the next village.

"You should get enough to last you until you're safely across the border," she explained. "Find yourself a monastery somewhere. It's what you've always wanted, isn't it?"

Alexander was too shocked to say anything. He just looked at her with his brow furrowed and his mouth slightly open as if waiting for words to emerge. Fausta's guilt was showing, and she must have felt it because she hardened her expression to compensate.

"I am doing this for your own good," she explained. "We both know you aren't suited to this."

"Good bye, sister," was all Alexander said in that moment. However, several hours later, as he followed the road away from the capital city, he formulated a better response in his mind.

I suppose having me beaten, humiliated, and condemned was for my own good too?

If he really wanted to make her angry, he may have added that she was no better than Justin. He sighed. Why did he always think of the right response in the wrong moment? He thought of several more, each he liked better than the last. He kicked himself for not thinking of them sooner.

He walked adjacent to the road at a distance to avoid being seen by other travelers. He doubted anyone would recognize him in his current state, but he didn't want to take the chance. The least his sister could have done was given him a cloak and shoes.

He ran the end of a long stick through the brush ahead of him, hoping it would frighten any snakes that lay hidden among the rocks. In the dark, it was impossible to see where he was putting his feet, and the brambles and stones cut into them as he walked.

Somehow, Fausta's rescue infuriated him. If she had him killed, he could have assumed that she hated him pure and simple. Her rescue proved that she did care for him, just not as much as ruling Kalathea. She made it very clear that if he was caught before he crossed the border, she couldn't do anything to protect him. He supposed mercy would ruin her image.

Maybe someday he'd return with an army of loyal followers, take back his kingdom, and see how she liked listening to an angry mob call for her head. Then he sighed. Who was he kidding? He wasn't going to take back his kingdom. He was going to do exactly what his sister told him to do. Leave Kalathea and become a monk. It sickened him to think that he was giving her what she wanted, but what else was he supposed to do? No one wanted him to be king, not even him.

He felt his stomach grumble and stopped brooding for a moment so he could think about food. Luckily, he saw the silhouettes of buildings ahead of him against the brightening horizon. Where there was a village, there was something to eat. He approached cautiously, avoiding the road and instead slipped between the houses and shops that made up the town.

The warm and lovely smell of fresh baked bread caught his attention. He followed the scent through the winding streets until he came to a bakery. It looked like the baker was just preparing to open for the day. The folding door that covered the storefront was closed except for two panels.

The rest of the shops along the street were closed completely, and Alexander couldn't see or hear anyone. He crept across the cobblestone street and cautiously peered through the opening in the door. The place was empty but it wouldn't be for long. There was a fire in the oven, and sitting out on one of the countertops was a basket of freshly baked loaves.

It occurred to Alexander that he was about to steal from a villager. It gave him an awful feeling. Perhaps his situation was dire enough to justify stealing; even so, some poor slave would probably get blamed for it and take a beating on his account. He couldn't live with that.

He thought of trading Fausta's necklace somewhere, and coming back later to buy the bread, but that would mean being seen and potentially recognized. At last he decided to take a loaf, and leave the chain from the necklace in payment. So he removed and pocketed the pendant, crept into the shop, and withdrew the smallest of the loaves. As he went to leave the chain on the table, a firm hand snatched his wrist.

"The sun's barely up and I've already caught a thief. This is going to be a long day."

The speaker was a woman. Everything about her was orderly. Her light brown hair was neatly pinned up beneath a veil. Though the surrounding surfaces were dusted with flour, there wasn't a speck on her clothing. Her presence was commanding, and Alexander wished he would drop dead rather than continue to endure her formidable gaze.

He tried to jerk his wrist out of her grip, but her hand remained unmoved. She was unusually strong for a woman. He jerked his wrist again. She was unusually strong for a human being. He got the impression she could snap his wrist with a flick of her own.

Since he could not retreat, he had no choice but to defend himself.

"I am not a thief," he blurted and immediately realized that, under the circumstances, it was the stupidest thing he ever said.

"Really?" the woman replied, a glimmer of amusement in her eye. "Just popped in to make sure everything was in order?"

He had no idea what to say. Every excuse that came to mind was ridiculous, so he settled on the truth. He looked at his feet, prayed silently for a moment, then said: "I came in to take the bread, but I am no thief. I was going to leave this in payment." He nodded to the chain in his hand.

The woman released him, took the chain, and held it up for inspection.

"Do you have a name, kid?" she asked.

"Pri— Kin—just, um, Alexander," he stuttered and immediately decided he surpassed the stupidity threshold he set a moment earlier.

"Well, Alexander," the woman replied. "My name is Eda. I am no thief either, but that is exactly what I would be if I only gave you a bit of bread in exchange for this."

She took a few coins from her pocket and placed them in his hand.

"Fair enough?" she asked.

Alexander remained petrified like a rabbit in the shadow of a hawk. For some reason, he was feeling distrustful lately, and couldn't convince himself that she was actually letting him go.

"Alright, fine!" she grumbled and placed another coin in his hand. "But you strike a hard bargain, my friend!"

"Why..." he began, but he wasn't sure what he was asking. Why was she letting him go? Why was she showing him kindness? Why did she believe him?

"You know, I'm not sure," she replied as though reading his mind. "I suppose it's because I've decided I like you, Alexander. And that's a high compliment because I don't like many people. Now I'm sure you have somewhere to be, off you go!"

Alexander scurried away feeling slightly less discouraged but no less confused.

5

Fairy Godmother Ex Machina

He'll be fine. Fausta told herself over and over again. All she wanted was to stop thinking about Alexander. She had saved the kingdom and she knew that he would be alright. She had to remind herself that he wasn't a child anymore. He would make himself a good life somewhere and be happy. He didn't need her watching over him, and besides she was a queen now with more important duties to attend too.

She wished there was some way she could learn what happened to him. For a brief moment, she thought of asking her genie companions. Then she rebuked herself for even entertaining the idea.

She was actually eager to be done with them. Without a coup to plan, she couldn't distract herself from the unpleasant feeling she got when they were around. So on the morning of Alexander's escape, she arranged to meet with them in a secluded corner of the garden. She thanked them for their assistance and tried to dismiss them.

"Go free?" Acacia asked. "You don't understand, My Queen. We genies are only happy when we are living in the service of a mortal."

Jace snorted and brought his fist to his mouth in an attempt to conceal the involuntary curl of his lips.

"Why, without a master we wander without purpose," Acacia continued. "It's a torturous existence."

"But I do not need anything from you," Fausta replied. "You'll find no purpose in serving me."

"A satisfied human?" Jace questioned. "How unusual!"

"I think she's trying to get rid of us, Jace," Acacia asserted.

Fausta's eyes widened in horror and she knelt before them.

"Do not be offended!" she begged. "I only want to make it clear that you are no longer indebted to me. With your magic, you could do anything, go anywhere! Why would you want to stay in Kalathea?"

"It's alright, My Queen," Acacia sighed. "I am sure we can find another master to serve. Jace, can you think of anyone who might need our services?"

"Hmm…" Jace thought. "We should find someone hopeless, friendless, someone with problems so great only magic can resolve them."

"I just thought of someone!" Acacia exclaimed. "How about Alexander?"

Fausta felt a knot in her stomach. "Then again," she answered slowly. "Running a kingdom is no easy task; I am sure I can find something for you to do."

The twins shared a smile.

As Alexander left the village, he noticed a beggar woman sitting by the road. She was asleep, curled up under her mantle. A clay bowl rested right by her face. She looked as if she was being crushed under the weight of some invisible burden. Alexander felt that even with all his recent misfortunes, her suffering was greater than his. He took one of the coins he had in his pocket, placed it in her bowl, and continued on his way.

After a few hours of walking, his steps became more difficult, and it took a conscious effort to keep his eyes open. It occurred to him that he'd hardly slept at all the night before.

When he could no longer force himself to press on, he found a clump of boulders and lay down behind them, hoping he would be concealed from view.

The roadside was hardly a substitute for his bed at the Kalathean palace, but he was so weary, he was asleep the moment he closed his eyes.

And as he slept, a memory returned to him in a dream. Justin was chasing him through the palace in a drunken rage. Alexander was convinced his brother was going to kill him this time.

His only chance of survival was finding his father. Just around the corner, there was a corridor, which would take him to the throne room and safety. Upon rounding the bend, he found his way blocked by a solid wall. Desperately, he drummed his fists against the wall, as if it would make the missing passageway reappear.

Justin was nearly upon him. Alexander turned to face him as he raised his blade to strike. Suddenly, a hand caught Justin's wrist. Fausta was standing between her brothers as if she'd materialized by magic.

"Don't you dare," she hissed to her elder brother. "I'll tell Father. He'll disinherit you. You'll be banished to the desert, where you will wander poor and starving, until death overtakes you and the vultures pick your bones clean."

Fausta always knew what to say.

Then, Justin vanished and Fausta was facing him. She looked at him with eyes full of compassion. It was like there was a small gap in his memory, he wasn't sure if Justin walked away, or disappeared into thin air. In his dream state, he didn't question it.

"Are you alright, little brother?" she asked.

He nodded. He suddenly realized she was kneeling down to look him in the eye, meaning it must have been a very old memory. She put a gentle hand on his cheek.

"Everything is going to be alright," she assured. "You're safe with me, understand?"

Alexander nodded.

Then, in an instant, she snatched her dagger with her opposite hand and swung it into his side.

Alexander jerked awake to a kick in the ribs.

"On your feet, kid!"

The speaker was a Kalathean guardsman. He was one of two who stood over him with weapons drawn. Alexander froze in an attempt to blend in with his surroundings.

"We can do this two ways, kid," the first guardsman continued. "You can resist, in which case we'll kill you, or you can surrender peacefully and we will take you back to Lysandria so they can kill you properly."

Alexander stood slowly, choosing the latter option.

"You know if we drag him all the way back to the capital, we're going to be stuck there until tomorrow," the fellow guardsman complained.

"Ugh, you're right," answered the first. "Do you think we'd get in trouble if we just killed him now and sent his head back?"

"Why would we? The outcome will be the same, won't it?"

The first considered this.

"If anyone asks," whispered the second. "He went into a rage and almost killed us."

"It was us or him," agreed the first.

The second guard forced him down onto his knees. Alexander found himself unable to move or think. He was gripped in the terror of the moment.

Luckily, as the first guard raised his blade, he was struck with that unexplainable paralysis that comes over people who try to kill the hero of an incomplete story. In that very same moment, someone spoke.

"That's an innocent man you're about to kill."

The speaker was the beggar woman from the village. She looked different somehow. She was standing tall and confident, the weight lifted from her shoulders. She held Alexander's captors at bay with her gaze. She had a sparkle in her eye and the slightest smirk on her lips.

"Madam," the first guard replied with a respect that seemed uncanny for a guard to give a beggar. "This boy is a dangerous criminal."

"You're mistaken," she asserted. "I know him quite well. He's a friend of mine."

"Not that well; he killed a man!"

The guard had lowered his weapon in a motion that seemed involuntary and stood unusually still.

"Really?" The woman answered. "How do you know it was him?"

"Well, he matches the description," the man answered, "right down to the slash above his eye."

"What slash?" the woman asked.

The guard stumbled forward as though he'd suddenly pulled himself free of snare. He grabbed a fist-full of Alexander's hair and brushed his bangs aside with the tip of his blade. He stared at Alexander's forehead for an uncomfortably long moment before releasing him.

"I suppose he doesn't," was the guard's dazed reply. He looked toward his fellow, who shrugged.

"Do me a favor?" the woman asked. "Next time you go to decapitate someone, please double check and make sure you have the right person."

"Of course, madam," the guard agreed. The two continued on their way in silence, occasionally glancing at each other and then back toward Alexander with baffled expressions.

Alexander slowly raised his hand to his forehead. Where he expected to feel the cruel wound, he touched healthy skin. Perhaps it was the shock of his inexplicable healing, or maybe it was the slow realization that he'd just escaped death for the second time that day, but he was suddenly feeling very light headed.

"Sit down! Sit down!" the woman urged. She ran to him and taking him by the arm, helped him sink down so he was sitting with his back against one of the boulders.

"Who are you?" he asked.

"My name is Alika," she replied. "I'm your godmother."

"My..." Alexander started, and then his eyes started to close and he almost fell face forward into her arms.

She shoved him back against the rocks. "Keep your eyes open," she ordered. "Swooning isn't princely!"

"I'm not…" Alexander began and started to fall forward again.

"Oh for goodness sake," Alika sighed, shoving him back against the boulder. "What am I doing? Surely I can fix a little fatigue!"

Alexander's head suddenly cleared and his energy returned and he leapt up and stumbled backward away from Alika, with eyes wide as saucers.

"My godmother?" he exclaimed. He had so many questions. Where had she been all his life? Why was she a beggar now? What kind of a trick was this? Instead of asking any of them, he stood staring at her with his mouth hanging slightly open.

"We'll explain everything soon enough, Your Majesty," Alika replied. "For now, I want you to continue on your way until you reach the monastery on Cedar Hill. You'll be safe there."

Alexander's expression did not change.

"Don't be afraid. We're looking after you, understand?" she said.

Alexander slowly shook his head.

"Excellent! See you soon!" Alika answered and disappeared.

6

Justice, Love, and Whatever

It was dusk when Alexander arrived at the monastery. He was nearly asleep on his feet. He knocked on the door and asked the brother who answered if they had a place for a weary traveler.

The monk let him in and asked him to wait a moment in the courtyard. It was quiet, except for the bubbling of the fountain in the center. The silence enveloped him like a warm blanket. He wished he could hide away there forever. Alexander leaned against one of the pillars that surrounded the courtyard and closed his eyes. He might have fallen asleep, if he hadn't heard a shuffling.

He looked up to see a bent old monk crossing the courtyard with a crate full of books. His skin was a very deep brown, almost black, and he had a massive grey beard. He was thin and frail and Alexander marveled that he was able to lift the box at all.

He forgot his weariness for a moment and approached the man.

"Let me take that for you," he offered.

The old man smiled warmly. "Thank you, son!"

He tossed the box into his arms. Alexander almost stumbled over backward when he caught it. Did books really weigh so much or was the old monk hiding an anvil in there somewhere?

"This way! This way!" the monk beckoned as he trotted along ahead. Alexander boosted the crate higher in his arms and struggled after him. The monk held a door open and waited for Alexander to catch up.

As Alexander passed him into the room, the old man said: "To what do I owe this honor, My King?"

Alexander turned white and dropped the crate. Its contents scattered in all directions.

"Be careful, Your Majesty," the monk rebuked. "These manuscripts are priceless."

"Um… you're mistaken," Alexander answered as he scrambled to collect the books. "Not about the books; I mean about me."

The monk chuckled. "Certainly not; I never forget a face."

Alexander turned red. He had no idea who the old monk was. He frequently forgot faces and names, and when he did remember them, he'd put the wrong name to the wrong face and embarrass himself.

"My name is Brother Joseph. I came with the abbot to visit your father a few years ago, though I am sure you don't remember; we only met briefly," said the monk.

"Oh," Alexander replied, glancing back across the courtyard to the main gate. "So… um… the abbot knows me too?"

"Certainly!" Joseph replied. "He's a close friend of your father's. He told us you were going to join us when you were old enough."

"Ah… right…" Alexander answered crawling under a bench to retrieve a book. "But, um, Father got sick, and asked me to wait a year." He set the book back in the crate. "And then he named me heir, and then he…" Alexander was horrified when he felt a tear on his cheek. "…And then I became king." He wiped his eye with his wrist and picked up the crate. "Where do you want this?"

The old monk motioned through the door. "Just put them anywhere," he said.

The door opened onto a little dining room. Alexander dropped the crate on the table and turned back toward the exit. "Well, brother, if that's all, I think I'd better get back to…um… running the kingdom."

"I am not going to hand you over, if that's what you're worried about," Joseph answered.

Alexander paused. News traveled fast.

"How do I know that?" he asked, his cheeks flushing red.

"You don't," Joseph answered. "If you'd rather not take the chance, the gate is right over there." He motioned to the other side of the courtyard.

Alexander was too confused and exhausted to know what to do. He sank down in one of the chairs and buried his head in his hands.

"Why wouldn't you turn me over? You've nothing to gain by protecting me," he cried.

"Because you didn't kill Justin," Joseph answered.

"I may as well have."

"What do you mean by that?" the old monk inquired.

"There was this brief moment," Alexander answered looking up from his palms. "As the shock of the grisly sight subsided, but before the people entered, when I felt…" he buried his face in his hands again, "relieved. Tell me, brother, what kind of person feels relief at the death of another?"

"One who's been living in fear of the dead man in question," Joseph answered.

"I'm a monster," Alexander mumbled.

"No," Brother Joseph replied. "You're a human. You know something? It might be a mercy if the guards find you here. They can't possibly be as cruel to you as you are to yourself."

"But, even before Justin's death, I was an awful king. Everything you've heard about me is true."

"You readopted the religion of our ancestors and started sacrificing peasants to Dythis?"

"Um, no?"

"You entertained your dinner guests by drowning kittens?"

"Um, what have you heard about me?"

"Lots of things, but since none of them seem to be true, tell me yourself what you did that was so terrible?"

"I was incompetent," Alexander continued. "When the Senate proposed a law, I was paralyzed with indecision. How could I possibly sign something when I didn't understand its effects? The Senate hated me, the people hated me, and rightly so. I failed them."

"You read everything you signed?" Joseph marveled.

"I haven't signed anything," Alexander answered. "I am still working through the first one. It's twelve hundred pages long."

"You're an awful politician," Joseph smiled. "But I think one day you'll make an excellent king."

Alexander lay his head down on the table and closed his eyes.

"Would it be alright if I slept a bit while we are waiting for the guards to come collect me?"

Joseph chuckled. "Let me go see if they've found a bed for you."

Alexander left early the next morning. He wanted to bid Brother Joseph goodbye but couldn't find him anywhere. None of his fellow monks seemed to know where he was, so Alexander left a message with them and departed.

He'd hardly started on his way when he saw the old man standing in the shade of a cedar. He was accompanied by two others. The first was the woman from the bakery. She was holding a scale. He saw a pile of gold coins on one side, but couldn't see what was on the other. Whatever it was must have been very heavy because that side was hanging lower.

The second person he didn't recognize… or maybe he did. He stared at her for several long moments before realizing that she was the beggar woman who saved him from the Kalathean guards.

She was completely transformed, her old rags replaced with a long white tunica. She was crowned with a golden diadem and clutching a sword in her left hand. Her weary, weatherworn face was now bright and beautiful. She reminded Alexander of one of the ancient goddesses. The intimidation he felt in her presence the day before was nothing compared to what he felt now.

"Eda, may I please have my scale back?" she was saying.

"No, Alika," Eda replied, scrutinizing the coins. "I'm not finished with it."

"He'll be here any moment," Alika protested.

"You know if you keep this up, the Council will expect you to be the justice fairy forever," Eda warned.

"I like being the justice fairy," Alika returned.

"I think you're going to frighten him," Joseph cautioned.

"Oh, I don't think so," Alika replied. "Mortals love the theatrics! Look, there he is now!"

She pointed in Alexander's direction. But he turned and tore back toward the monastery.

"Your Majesty! Please wait!" Alika called.

Alexander suddenly found himself frozen midstride. He couldn't move forward, but when he heard her approaching from behind, he found he could turn back toward her.

His face was white and he was trembling from head to foot. He gripped one hand in the other in a futile attempt to stop the shaking. Then, he looked Alika in the eye and said, "I'll—I'll have you know. That I am a Christian, so if it's worship you want, you'll have to um… go elsewhere. I am of no use to you so you might as well um, just let me go, please."

"He's adorable," Eda remarked. "Can we keep him?"

Alika shot her a glare. "We're not gods, Your Majesty," she corrected. "We're fairies."

Alexander glanced at each of them. "Fairies?"

"Yes, I am Alika the Fairy of Justice."

"I am Eda, and I like to keep my options open."

Alika elbowed her in the ribs.

"Fine," Eda growled. "I am the Fairy of..." she twirled her hand in the air, searching for the right word, "how about prudence?"

"You already know me," Joseph smiled. "I am the Fairy of Love."

Alexander stared at him blankly. He looked exactly the same as he had the evening before: a bent old man, with callused hands, a gentle smile, and a glimmer in his eye.

"You're a fairy too?" he questioned.

Joseph nodded.

"Of love?"

Brother Joseph nodded again.

Alexander regarded him.

"What were you expecting, Aphrodite?" Eda smirked.

"I am so confused," Alexander complained and then looked back to Alika. "Didn't you say you were my godmother?"

"Yes, fairies can also be godparents, you know," Alika affirmed. "And that reminds me."

She sheathed her sword and a wooden box appeared in her hands. She gave it to Alexander. Inside were a candle and a tiny white gown.

"That's been in my sock drawer for the last sixteen years; it's time you had it back," Alika said.

"Thank you?" Alexander replied.

"And we have a few more gifts for you," Eda said, holding out the scale so he could see what was outweighing the gold. It was a chain and a single coin.

"Do you recognize them?" Eda asked. "The gold opposite is all the money Fausta offered to the poor in Justin's name."

Alexander regarded the items with his brow furrowed.

"What does that tell you?" Joseph asked.

"That the chain must be incredibly dense," Alexander answered, poking it curiously.

"Yes," Eda sighed. "Just like a certain king I know."

"What king?" Alexander asked.

"Why did you give me that chain?" Eda continued, changing the subject.

"I didn't want to steal, I mean, not when I had something I could give in return," Alexander muttered.

"Is that all?"

Alexander shrugged. "I thought someone else might get blamed for taking it."

"You considered how your actions would affect other people," Eda asserted. "And because of that, I am going to give you a swamp."

"...A swamp?" Alexander asked.

"Yes," a scroll appeared in Eda's hand. She gave it to Alexander. "There's the deed."

"Thank you," Alexander replied. In that moment, he decided there wasn't any point in questioning anything anymore.

"And because you considered my misfortune before your own," Alika added. "I am going to give you what was taken from you—a good name. From this day forward, you will be known for your wisdom and kindness, not here in Kalathea, mind you, but in your new home in Kaltehafen."

"Kaltehafen?" Alexander mumbled. "Wait a moment; that's a barbarian kingdom, isn't it?"

"Don't worry, Your Majesty, we won't make you walk there," Alika said and smiled.

And just like that, Alexander found himself someplace entirely different. The air was crisp and cold and the sky was blanketed with grey clouds. He was standing in a clearing amidst a forest of towering evergreens. The grass was muddy, and here and there across the clearing and among the trees, he could see frozen pools.

He was grateful to see that his attire had changed to combat frigid weather. He had a hat, a warm cloak, a longer tunic, and hose. He looked down at himself and realized to his horror that he was dressed like a barbarian. He sighed, at least he was warm. The three fairies remained exactly as they were. How Alika wasn't freezing to death without sleeves was a mystery to him.

"Welcome home!" Eda smiled gesturing toward a ramshackle house on the edge of the wood. "Inside, you'll find everything you need to get you through the winter. Cozy, isn't it? And it's only half a day's walk from the capital city."

"I am grateful for your help," Alexander answered, glancing anxiously around the frozen wood. "But, um, I was hoping I wouldn't have to go quite this far from home."

"This is the safest place for you," Alika explained.

"Besides, in the spring, you'll find there's gold in this swamp," Eda smiled. She was looking exceptionally pleased with herself.

Suddenly, a third woman appeared beside Alika.

"Ah, there you are, Alika! I have an urgent message for you from the Fairy High Council," the newcomer stated.

"I am speaking with a mortal right now. Can it wait?" she asked back.

"Afraid not, the king of the high elves is threatening to commit genocide again, and the council wants you to talk him out of it."

"Really? Again?" Alika exclaimed. "He's just being dramatic, you know. He's not actually going to do it."

"I'm just the messenger," the newcomer shrugged. "You're going to have to take it up with the Council."

Alika rolled her eyes and grumbled something under her breath. "I am so sorry, Your Majesty. I have to go. Everything is going to be alright; trust me," she said and then looked to Joseph and added, "Aphrodite, don't forget to warn him about the twins." Then, she disappeared.

"Twins?" Alexander asked.

"I'll explain in a moment," Joseph said. "But first, I haven't given you my gift yet! Because you forgot your own weariness to help me, I am going to give you something that will help you love, when love seems impossible."

Joseph withdrew a worn wooden crucifix from his pocket and placed it in Alexander's hand. "Now, let's go inside, we have a lot to talk about," he said.

The three sat on the floor around the fire. The house wasn't much more than four walls with a hole in the center of the roof for letting smoke escape. A makeshift fence divided off a portion. That section must have been for animals; there was an old manger attached to the fence and small heaps of straw here and there.

There, Brother Joseph and Eda did something fairies almost never do. They explained everything.

They told Alexander about how each fairy is tasked with bringing the good out of others and how Jace and Acacia abandoned that mission. They told him of their escape and how the plot to overthrow him was simply another one of their sadistic games.

Alexander listened to the entire story white-faced.

"Can't you recapture them?" Alexander questioned.

"When I realized they escaped, I informed the Fairy High Council immediately," Joseph answered. "They told me they received my concern and would handle the situation promptly."

"So we probably won't hear from them for a hundred and fifty years," Eda grumbled.

Alexander wondered if she was exaggerating. She didn't seem like she was exaggerating.

"Unfortunately, they aren't the only rogue fairies on the loose," Joseph continued. "The Council has its hands full."

Alexander went even paler. "How many—I mean, um, what makes them rebel?"

"Imagine spending your each and every day offering people the opportunity to act selflessly, knowing that they won't," Eda explained.

"How do you know they won't?" Alexander asked.

"When you've been doing this as long as I have, you can tell," Eda answered. "Take Alika's elf king for example. He's always been a stubborn, conceited, sanctimonious—"

"*Eda*," Joseph warned.

Eda gave an irritated little sigh. "A thousand years from now, he'll be exactly the same. Alika knows it and yet when the Council says 'make him see reason' she dutifully follows orders every single time."

"How discouraging," Alexander mumbled.

"You have no idea," Eda agreed. "I'd be lying if I said I hadn't come close to giving up."

"So why don't you?" Brother Joseph smiled.

"Because for every hundred selfish souls, there is one person who sincerely longs to do the right thing, and just needs a little help figuring out what that right thing is. Those are the people who make it all worthwhile."

"Well," Alexander said. "I hope they assign you someone like that soon."

A smile flickered across her lips. "I am hopeful, Alexander. I really am."

They did not explain why they put Alexander in a swamp in Kaltehafen. When he inquired about it, they suddenly became much more fairylike and told him he would have to find out for himself.

7

Alexander Gets Kidnapped by a Princess

"How's the swamp?" Eda smirked.

It was spring. The air was finally warming and the forest was ablaze with colorful wildflowers. Despite this, Alexander had locked himself in his house and plugged every opening with old rags. If Eda hadn't materialized in the middle of the room, she would never have gotten in.

The swamp was infested with bees.

"It's... um... very pretty," he answered, forcing a smile. He picked up a piece of bark and scraped a stinger out of his arm. "Lots of flowers and um… lots of bees."

"Found any gold yet?" she asked, her smirk broadening.

He shook his head.

She looked at the swelling sting on his arm. "It seems to me, it found you." Then she glanced around the room. "You really should get some more candles, Your Majesty. It's dark in here."

"I wish you wouldn't speak in riddles," Alexander commented.

Eda looked offended. "Why do you always assume I am speaking in riddles?"

"Can I get you something?" Alexander sighed. He didn't know whether or not fairies needed to eat like humans but thought it polite to offer. "I don't have much left, um… I have some bread; it's a bit stale though."

Eda took a seat on an old crate. (Alexander didn't have any chairs.) "Stale bread isn't so bad if you put a little honey on it."

Alexander raised an eyebrow. Why would she think he had honey? Peasants didn't have honey. It was rare and expensive. His mouth fell open.

"Why, Alexander," Eda said. "You look as if you've just solved a riddle! It's about time; that was excruciating."

Alexander had no idea how to extract the honey from the bee hives, but Eda promised she would send someone to help him. The next day, a band of lost friars knocked on his door. They'd come to ask for directions, but when they saw bee hives they started jumping up and down and singing *Te Deum*.

He had a bit of trouble communicating with them as he couldn't speak Kaltic and, while they did know Latin, they had very thick accents. Eventually, they managed by passing notes. (All educated Kalts used Latin for writing since their native written language consisted of only five runes and was therefore useless for practical conversation.)

The friars were destined for the nearby monastery of St. Loudon, and when they arrived there, they told their fellows about the wonderful discovery in Alexander's swamp. The abbot immediately sent two of his own, Brother Joseph the Elder and Brother Joseph the Younger, to assist with the bees. (Alexander couldn't help but smile when they introduced themselves, wondering if he would ever befriend a monk who wasn't named Joseph.) All through the summer, the Josephs came and went, first showing Alexander how to extract the honey, and then showing him how to make candles and soaps out of beeswax. They also helped him improve his Kaltic. He had a gift for learning languages and was fluent in no time at all.

Alexander would periodically load a cart with the goods they produced and take them into the city to sell. The local merchants noticed that he was fair and straightforward, and the friars loved him for his diligence. He was a new and exciting face. The townsfolk spoke of him frequently, commenting on his knowledge, generosity, and manners.

As Alika promised, his reputation flourished. He became known in the city as Alexander the Greek. He tried to correct this at first, but soon realized that most of the townsfolk were uneducated. He doubted any of them could find Kalathea on a map. It didn't help that Greek was his first language. Supposedly, Kalatheans had a language of their own in ages past, but no one could remember it. In the ancient world, stealing culture from the Greeks was something of a fad and the Kalatheans did not want to be left out. Of course, after over a millennium of linguistic evolution, Kalathean Greek was a bit different.

When the bees returned the second year, Alexander was prepared for them. His skills improved, he sold more, and he gained more confidence. When he needed help, he went to visit the friars.

He made a decent living for himself and decided to use some of his earnings to take up painting again. When he was a prince, this was his favorite pastime. He spent the winter mixing colors by candlelight. His art was mostly the faces of the saints, but now and then he diverged, immortalizing the faces of other people. He started to paint his parents, but had to imagine how his mother looked since she died when he was a baby. When he realized she probably looked like Fausta, he left that painting unfinished.

The third year came and went and Alexander realized that he was comfortable and content. He never imagined becoming a candle maker, but it was certainly better than being a king. Still, he had a hole in his heart. He was respected by everyone but did not have any close friends. Not a soul knew who he really was and keeping that secret made him feel isolated.

On a cold afternoon during the fourth autumn, he pushed his cart along the road to the city. It was to be his last load that year. The sky was heavy with grey clouds and he prayed it wouldn't snow until he returned home.

He suddenly heard hooves thundering behind him.

"STOP!" a woman called.

Alexander dropped the cart and swung around in alarm. Two riders halted before him. The first, a lady of royal blood, adorned in colorful raiment and jewelry. A crown circled her head, atop her white veil. The second was a mountain of a warrior, likely the woman's guard.

Alexander bowed respectfully.

"Are you Alexander the Greek?" she demanded.

"I am," he answered.

"Excellent! Egbert, grab him," she ordered.

"Sorry, what—" but before Alexander could finish speaking, the warrior rode up behind him, grabbed him by the shoulder, lifted him onto his horse, and sent the animal charging forward.

"Who are you? What is the meaning of this?" Alexander demanded.

"I am Princess Ilona!" she cried galloping after him. "Sister of King Florian of North Kaltehafen and King Filbert of the South! I require your services!"

"I am a free citizen!" Alexander protested. "And I demand you stop immediately and explain yourself!"

"Citizen?" Ilona laughed. "How like a Greek!"

"I am a Kalathean!" Alexander retorted indignantly.

"Same thing!" she returned.

"No! Not remotely!" Alexander snapped. "I thought a lady of your status would know that! I forget you're still a barbarian."

She slowed her horse a bit so she was riding parallel to Egbert and looked at Alexander with a devilish grin.

"That's exactly what a Greek would say!"

Alexander's mouth dropped open for a moment, and then his face went scarlet. "How dare you!" he started, but she charged on ahead. "You kidnap me! You insult me! You can't—" He continued calling after her but she did not respond. He finally ceased calling and started brooding silently. Getting kidnapped by a princess was the pinnacle of humiliation.

At last, they came to an open plain. Alexander could see a battle encampment in the distance. He prayed that it wasn't their destination. God heard his prayer but ignored it.

Ilona rode straight into the midst of the soldiers and dismounted. Egbert halted just behind and dropped Alexander on the ground. He leapt to his feet, hoping to retain whatever dignity he had left.

A knight with a massive blue plume in his helmet greeted Ilona with a low bow.

"Princess," he said. "You shouldn't be here."

"I need to speak with my brother, it's urgent," she replied.

"Of course," the knight answered. "I will tell him you're here."

"Well?" Alexander demanded. His arms were crossed and he was scowling at the princess. "Are you going to explain yourself?"

"My stupid brothers are fighting again! I brought you here so you could talk some sense into them!"

Alexander stared at her blankly.

She sighed. "Last month, Filbert came to stay at Castle Erkscrim so we could all celebrate the harvest festival together. There we were, enjoying the feast like a peaceful, respectable family, when Filbert mentions that he's been reading the philosopher Severinus and agrees with his theory that the entire universe is made up of triangles. Then, Florian answered that he'd been reading Caius and that the universe is actually made up of nautilus spirals."

Alexander rolled his eyes. "That's a massive oversimplification. Rouvin later clarified that the movable elements are made of nautilus spirals and the immovable elements are made up of triangles."

"THAT'S EXACTLY WHAT I TRIED TO TELL THEM!" Ilona exclaimed.

"Wait, you've read Rouvin?" Alexander asked, his scowl shrinking slightly.

"Of course, I've read Rouvin!" she snapped. "I'm not completely ignorant, you know!"

"So why wouldn't they listen to you?"

"Because women are incapable of reason," she replied.

"So they've read some Rouvin, too," Alexander mumbled thoughtfully. "But why me? Couldn't you send any other man in to talk to them?"

"I've heard that you are knowledgeable on such matters. The friars speak very highly of you, you know," she said.

"If I talk to your brothers, will you let me go home?"

"Of course I will."

"Alright," Alexander grumbled. "I'll talk to them, but I can't promise it will change anything AND I expect full payment for anything in my cart I find damaged or missing on my return."

She laughed. "My brothers may be idiots, but they are very dear to me. If you save them, I will give you anything your heart desires."

Having pointless philosophical arguments was how aristocrats entertained themselves in the Middle Ages. And like many who entertain themselves in this way, the kings knew a little about philosophy but thought they knew a lot.

Ilona finally convinced the two of them to sit down with Alexander in Florian's camp. Alexander had to look back and forth between them a number of times to make sure his vision was correct. They were identical twins. He was grateful Florian had a beard or he would have lost track of which was which.

He stayed with them long into the night, gently asking them questions and directing their thoughts. Each time one brother became enraged, it only took a few patient words from Alexander to calm him. When the dawn came, the brothers left the tent laughing together.

"You have enlightened me, Alexander!" Florian exclaimed, giving him a slap on the back that sent him stumbling forward. "The movable elements! It makes so much sense!"

Ilona rolled her eyes and muttered several unladylike words under her breath.

"To think, we almost killed each other!" Filbert admitted.

Florian slapped his hand on Filbert's shoulder. "I've been trying to kill you since before I was born!" They both dissolved into laughter.

Ilona was not amused.

"No more philosophy," she insisted. "I don't like what it does to you two."

Alexander bowed deeply to the kings. "If there is nothing more I can do for Your Majesties, I really must be getting back to my cart."

"You can't leave now!" Florian exclaimed. "You must come back to castle Erkscrim! My brother and I are going to throw a feast to celebrate the restoration of our friendship!"

"Oh no," Ilona breathed. She grabbed Alexander's arm. "My brother is right! You will be our guest of honor! We will seat you right between our two kings!"

He jerked away from her. She had no boundaries and it irritated him.

"I can't—" Alexander began, sending an anxious glance toward the cloudy sky.

She slipped a coin purse into Alexander's hand and hissed: "Don't worry about the cart. The security of the kingdom is at stake!"

The feast triggered memories of the Kalathean palace. So many faces all talking at once, so many unwritten social rules to remember. Alexander didn't like feasts—well, he liked the food, just not the atmosphere. He was surrounded by people and yet felt completely alone. The feast at Erkscrim was worse than the ones in Kalathea because he only knew the hosts (and them only a little).

He was also horrified to discover that the rumors about the Kalts letting dogs into their dining halls were true. The hounds patrolled the tables, snapping up scraps that fell onto the floor. The Kalts seemed to find their begging endearing and would reward them generously. Alexander found the whole thing unsanitary.

He jumped when he felt something touching him from under the table, and looked down to see one of the creatures resting its head on his knee. It was a large black dog with a short coat, floppy ears, and giant brown sorrowful eyes—eyes that looked like they had witnessed a thousand tragedies. (They were actually very much like Alexander's.)

"Um, hello, dog," he greeted, bringing a hesitant hand toward its nose. This had to be deception. He was sure he was going to lose a finger, but he couldn't help reaching out toward the velvety snout.

"Hey, Lanzo!" Ilona shouted, giving the dog's face a swat. "Leave him alone! Away with you!"

The animal disappeared under the table cloth.

"Don't let Lanzo fool you," Ilona warned. "He's as deceptive as he is greedy, and he's had plenty tonight."

Alexander looked across the room. Lanzo was lying in the corner with his head on his forepaws looking at him with those gentle, soul-swallowing eyes. Alexander looked away in an attempt to ease the guilt in his heart. He tried to focus on the conversations taking place around him.

Filbert and Florian loved quoting the philosophers and did so liberally. Their actual understanding of the philosophy was superficial. When they spoke, he felt embarrassed for them. Then there was Ilona. She wasn't able to add much to their discussion because they kept talking over her and interrupting.

This irritated Alexander because he was sincerely interested in her opinion. He wasn't sure who she had read or how much, but she seemed to have an understanding that her brothers lacked.

When the feast was drawing to a close, she stepped away. Alexander followed her, eager for an excuse to get out. He found her looking out into the bailey at the heavy snowfall. Her face was white with horror.

"Is everything alright?" Alexander asked.

"Look at that snow," she said. "It's been falling heavier and heavier. Do you know what that means?"

Alexander shook his head.

"It means Filbert can't leave tomorrow! And if this winter is anything like the last, it's only going to keep snowing, and we won't be rid of him until spring!"

She looked at Alexander with an exasperated expression. "If I have to be stuck in here with those two all winter, I am going to fling myself off the north tower!"

"It can't be that bad," Alexander answered, although he had enough experience with siblings to know that it could be. In fact, it could be a lot worse.

"My only consolation is that you are stuck here too! If you can't keep those two civil, no one can!"

Alexander's heart sank. His little house wasn't much but it was his own private space. His paints were there too. He hoped Ilona was wrong about the snow; otherwise he'd be imprisoned with strangers for months.

He told himself that at least it wouldn't be so damp, and the food would certainly be better, and Ilona made interesting conversation. Then, something wonderful occurred to him.

"Princess," he asked. "Do you have books here?"

Books were not something he could afford on a candle maker's salary. He had to go to the friary when he wanted to read.

"Of course we do," she answered. "Follow me; I'll show you the library."

Alexander's heart skipped. He could tolerate almost anything for the sake of books.

8

Modern Architecture

The library was a tiny, windowless room containing one chair, a shallow desk, and about thirty books. Twenty of them, the princess owned personally and the others were loaned from the friary. Ilona explained that she exchanged them with the friars when she wanted something new.

Alexander felt a twinge of jealousy. The friars never let him take books home. He had to sit in their library until he finished reading. He could tell which ones belonged to the friars because they had a little hole in the binding where they had been chained to the shelves. This was to keep visitors from succumbing to temptation and making off with them. Alexander supposed getting to borrow books was one of the privileges of being royalty.

To Alexander, that little room was paradise. He forgot that he was angry with Ilona for kidnapping him and sat with her late into the evening, talking and poring over different texts. As the night wore on, their conversation became less and less intelligent and everything became amusing, and they found themselves laughing together at absolutely nothing.

The days came and went, one after another and Alexander was the happiest he'd ever been. He wasn't sure why; he had books back in Kalathea, a lot more books, better books. What he didn't have was a close friend. Ilona was intelligent and adventurous, and had a bold, slightly irreverent sense of humor. He spent every possible moment in her company.

She often spoke of her brothers, which made Alexander aware of two things: first that she adored them and second that she was always on the verge of strangling them.

"I've never seen them agree about anything except that I should be locked away in a cloister," she complained one day. "I escaped three times before the Mother Superior refused to take me back."

Alexander was sitting on the floor of the library, with his back to the wall and an ecclesiastical history open on his lap. Lanzo was lying on the floor at his feet, resting his sorrowful head on Alexander's ankles. The creature had taken a liking to him, and made a habit of following him wherever he went.

He glanced up at Ilona. (She was occupying the only chair in the room.) It seemed to him that her deep understanding of the scriptures and philosophy made her an ideal candidate for the convent.

"But why?" he asked. "You'd have made such an excellent nun."

"What's that supposed to mean?" she questioned.

Alexander blushed. He paused trying to figure out why his previous statement warranted such a reaction.

"I… um…" he stuttered, trying to buy himself some time while he contemplated the error of his words. "I mean that you are so pious."

"So piety is reserved for the consecrated in the Greek church?" she grinned. "And you say we're unorthodox."

"No, but um…" Alexander struggled desperately to grasp the words that would save him. "I mean… um… you are such a deep thinker. Doesn't a life of contemplation appeal to you?"

"Certainly, but the cloister isn't my calling," she replied.

"Oh," Alexander answered, mulling over her words. As he understood it, your parents decided what your calling was. Long before he was born, his father and mother decided they were going to give their third child to the Church. Alexander never questioned their decision, but was ready to obey like a good son. In truth, he liked that the decision was made for him. He had plenty to worry about without having to decide what he wanted to do with his life.

"Um… How do you know it isn't your calling?" he asked.

"Because insanity is not becoming for a nun, and the longer I am cooped up the more my sanity wanes. Just wait a few more weeks, you'll see!"

Alexander's mind raced. The idea of choosing his own path in life was terrifying. More terrifying than being ordered to take the crown. He admired Ilona's courage. He wondered how she would make a decision like that.

"What will you do now?" Alexander pressed.

"Now that's a bold question," Ilona accused.

Alexander sighed. He was amazed she hadn't asked him to leave with the way he kept offending her. Despite her criticism, her expression was amused, not angry. It was almost like she enjoyed making him feel uncomfortable.

"I apologize," he said, and looked back to his book.

"But if you insist on knowing, I am building a cathedral," Ilona explained.

"You're what?" Alexander asked.

"Well, having one built," Ilona clarified. "I want to dedicate my life to doing something that will help the people, glorify God, and make every other kingdom feel inferior!"

She leapt up from her seat and withdrew a rolled piece of parchment from a chest next to the bookshelf. She beckoned for Alexander to come and look as she spread it on the table. It was a drawing of a magnificent structure. The bell towers were at least as high as Erkscrim's (assuming the drawing was to scale). What drew Alexander's attention immediately was the size of the windows. They seemed to take up a large portion of the outer wall, and he wondered how the building could stand with such vulnerability.

"Did you draw this?" Alexander asked.

Ilona laughed. "No, I've hired an architect from France. I've heard wonderful things about him. Of course, none of his churches will be completed in our lifetimes. I suppose my grandchildren will assess his talents properly. By the way!" she interjected. "You are going to paint the altarpiece!"

Alexander looked perplexed. How did she know about his painting?

"You painted St. John, didn't you? The one in the vestibule at St. Loudon's?" she asked.

"Oh yes," Alexander replied. "That was mine."

"You're wonderful!" Ilona stated. "And that's why I've chosen you."

Alexander tried not to let the exhilaration he was feeling show. He pressed his lips together to keep himself from slipping into a smile. "I doubt you'll be ready for an altarpiece in my lifetime."

Ilona waved off his objection. "Just do it before you die; your grandchildren can install it."

She stretched. It was late in the evening. Alexander hoped she wasn't thinking about going to bed. He was enjoying their conversation despite the fact that he kept embarrassing himself. He was relieved when she continued speaking.

"Tell me, why are you a candle maker when you can paint so well?"

"That's a long story," Alexander answered.

"The night is young," Ilona pushed.

"Well, my father was a governor back in Kalathea," Alexander began, crafting his words carefully. "And when I was born, he decided he would give me to the Church."

"Youngest child?" Ilona asked.

He nodded.

"Why do parents always give the Church their spare children?" she ranted. "Isn't that like throwing God the leftovers?"

"Leftovers?" Alexander objected indignantly. "Your Highness, we youngest children are the best our parents have to offer. We are the perfection of their art."

Illona giggled. "You've a brilliant mind!"

"In any case," Alexander continued. "I thought I should learn something that would be suited to the monastic life. So I learned to write icons, copy manuscripts, translate… that sort of thing. Then, my elder brother died unexpectedly, and I became my father's heir."

"I'm sorry," Ilona answered. "Did your brother die fighting?"

Alexander thought. "No, I don't think he ever saw it coming."

"Don't you have any family left?" she pressed.

"No," he answered. "My father died a few years ago and my mother died before I was born."

Ilona snorted in an attempt to conceal a laugh. It didn't work. The laugh burst forth and she turned bright red as she tried to stop herself. "I'm so sorry, Alex!" she cried. "It's not your parent's deaths—"

Alexander realized what he'd said and smiled sheepishly. "*After* I was born," he corrected.

"I know! I know! That's what you meant!" she answered. "I shouldn't have laughed, but you said it so seriously!"

"It's alright," Alexander smirked. "We both know you're a heartless person."

"You're never going to let me forget this, are you?" she said.

He shook his head, his smile broadening triumphantly. This made her laugh all the more.

Once she'd recovered herself, the conversation moved to other things. Alexander felt a twinge of guilt at leaving Fausta out of his story. These days, he avoided thinking about her, as if ignoring her existence would erase her betrayal.

9

A Brutal War

Alexander hated snow. They didn't have much snow in Kalathea. Flurries and hail every once in a while, but nothing like the Kaltic blizzards that buried everything in massive drifts. As a child, he would see snow on the mountain tops and dream about what it was like up close. He discovered, to his chagrin, that it was cold and wet and boring when you'd been staring at it for weeks on end.

Nothing could persuade him to leave the safety of the fireside and venture out into the bailey, nothing except Ilona. Even a castle as large as Erkscrim became a prison after weeks of confinement and Ilona was desperate to escape. She invited Alexander to accompany her. He tried to convince her to stay inside, but when he couldn't, followed her out.

He couldn't live with himself if she got lost and froze to death in some snowdrift. Of course, Egbert was with her. He was almost like an accessory. He followed whenever she left the castle, never saying a word, but growling at anyone or anything he viewed as a threat.

As the three of them passed through the doors, Ilona spotted her brothers standing a short distance away. She scooped up a handful of snow and kneaded it into a ball. Then, she threw it at Florian, hitting him square in the back of the head.

He looped around, but Ilona had ducked out of sight, leaving Egbert and Alexander as the only two suspects. Egbert pointed at Alexander. Before the latter realized he'd been framed, Filbert was holding him down while Florian was dumping armfuls of snow down the back of his tunic.

"Unhand him!" came Ilona's voice from somewhere above.

"Not until we've finished putting this insolent plebeian in his place!" Filbert objected.

Suddenly, the kings were subjected to a rain of snowballs so thick it blocked out the sunlight. Ilona had turned all the watchmen on the wall against them.

"Treacherous wench!" cried Florian from beneath the hail. The twins abandoned Alexander and fought their way toward the tower stairs. Ilona peered over the wall and called, "War is upon you, Greek! Best you decide where your loyalties lie."

"With you of course, Your Highness!" Alexander cried. He scooped up a fist full of snow and tore after the kings.

The Middle Ages was a brutal time, meaning that ice balls and shots to the face were not forbidden in snowball fights. It was a long and merciless war. In the end, no one was victorious. No one surrendered. The two armies dissolved into smaller factions, some returning to the warmth of the fires and some returning to their duties.

Alexander couldn't believe how warm he was when it ended considering he was soaked through. It was probably because he hadn't stopped running since the affair began. He stood next to Ilona on the upper wall, panting slightly as the warriors dispersed.

"You fought well," Ilona commented, "considering you still have much to learn about winter warfare."

"Like what?" Alexander questioned.

"Betrayal is always imminent," she answered, pelting a snowball into his nose.

She ran away laughing hysterically.

Alexander tore after her, snatching her by the hand as she tried to escape.

"How are your hands so warm!" she exclaimed. She turned toward him suddenly and took his opposite hand in hers. It was so cold Alexander marveled she could move it at all.

"You should go in," he suggested.

She shook her head. "I'd rather freeze to death then spend another moment in that prison."

She tightened her hands around his. He looked down at them. Normally, he jerked away when someone so much as brushed against him, but for some reason, he didn't mind Ilona's touch. It felt good, very good. He closed his fingers more tightly around hers and stood for a moment looking into her eyes.

Her wit always sparkled in her eyes. When he looked at them, he couldn't help but wonder what mischief she was planning. They were lovely eyes, such a clear blue. All the Kalts had blue eyes, but for some reason Alexander only noticed hers.

Standing there, hand in hand with her, drinking in her gaze was a wonderful feeling. It brought about a happiness that filled him completely. He paused. *Why?* He never experienced a feeling like it before. It was too wonderful to trust.

His own gloves were tucked into his belt. He released her hands and offered them to her.

"Thank you," she smiled before tossing them over the wall. Alexander watched as they tumbled into a snowdrift below.

"Why did you do that?" Alexander asked helplessly. She took his hands again.

"Because I like this better," she answered.

Alexander scrutinized her. He couldn't make any sense of her actions. He couldn't make any sense of his feelings. He couldn't make any sense of anything.

"Is this why Rouvin says that women are incapable of reason?" he wondered aloud.

Ilona scowled and jerked away from him. "If there's one thing I've learned from Rouvin, it's that the wisest men are often the most foolish."

She stormed away leaving Alexander thoroughly perplexed.

The next day, Ilona seemed to have forgotten the entire incident. She found Alexander early in the morning and asked him to accompany her on a walk. It was warm for the first time in weeks. The icicles that decorated the eaves dripped, causing a tiny rain shower around the perimeter of the roof. The snow had receded here and there, leaving muddy patches in its wake.

Alexander let himself absorb the sun's warm caress. It was like experiencing a little taste of Kalathea.

"Strange as it sounds," Ilona began. "I'm glad we are trapped here."

"Weren't you just complaining about being cooped up?" Alexander teased.

"Well, yes, but it could be so much worse you know," she continued. "You saved me, Alexander. I would have died of boredom if it wasn't for you. Brother Joseph was right to boast about you."

"Joseph the Younger or Joseph the Elder?" Alexander asked.

"Joseph the Dark," Ilona replied, casually.

Alexander furrowed his brow.

"I don't know him," he replied.

"You must know him," Ilona objected. "He's been there forever, at least as long as I can remember. He's my godfather, you know."

"I only know of two brother Josephs at St. Loudon's," Alexander answered.

"There are three," Ilona insisted. "The Younger, the Elder, and the Dark. I can't believe you haven't met him; he always answers the door for me."

"What does he look like?" Alexander tried. He wondered if he knew this third Joseph by a nickname. The friars had to have some way of differentiating their Josephs.

"He is the sweetest old man," Ilona answered. "He has the darkest skin of anyone I've ever seen."

Considering Ilona lived in a kingdom where most people were whiter than marble, this didn't mean much. He needed a reference.

"Darker than me?" he asked.

"Oh much darker," Ilona replied. "His skin is almost black. He's very thin and has a massive grey beard."

Now Alexander was thoroughly puzzled. She was describing the Brother Joseph he had met on his escape from Kalathea in the monastery on Cedar Hill. That Brother Joseph had no reason to be in St. Loudon's Monastery. That Brother Joseph wasn't even human.

"How is it possible that you don't know him?" Ilona wondered. "When he's always talking about you?"

Alexander had a suspicion that he did know this Brother Joseph but wasn't sure how to explain their relationship to Ilona. He didn't completely understand it himself. It seemed to him that this Brother Joseph was up to something; he wasn't exactly sure what.

Ilona must have noticed the confusion on his face because she said, "After the thaw, we'll go to St. Loudon's and resolve this."

"Yes," Alexander agreed. "I think that's an excellent idea."

She glanced around the courtyard at the muddy puddles and the dripping eves, and then her expression changed slightly. The amusement left her face, and her cheeks became slightly pink.

"You know, you don't have to leave after the thaw if you don't want to," Ilona said. "There isn't any hurry."

"Hmm?" Alexander glanced sideways at her.

"Unless you are still eager to get back to your cart," she grinned.

Alexander glanced around at the melting snow and felt his heart starting to sink. He would have to leave soon. He had candles to make and paintings to finish and his own private home waiting for him where he would be *alone*.

He smirked at the princess, attempting to ignore his heavy heart. "I think you mean *your* cart. You paid for it, remember? I don't know why you bought a cart only to leave it abandoned on the roadside all winter, but who am I to question a princess?"

Her smile broadened. Everything around her seemed to brighten when she smiled. Alexander wondered why he hadn't noticed it before.

"No one," she replied, "so hold your tongue."

10

A Horrifying Realization

Alexander couldn't sleep. He wondered if he would be able to see Ilona again once he left, then scolded himself for being presumptuous. She was a princess, not the type of person who would keep the company of a candle maker unless circumstances forced them together.

He left his room and wandered to the chapel. Perhaps God would help him make sense of his tangled thoughts. The halls were completely silent, so that his every footstep seemed loud enough to wake the whole castle. He tried shuffling his feet. It was only slightly better.

As he entered the chapel, he was surprised to see Ilona kneeling silently before an image of the Virgin Mary. She seemed deeply absorbed in meditation, so Alexander slipped quietly to the opposite side of the church.

He tried to focus on his prayers, but his gaze kept drifting over to her. He wondered what colors he would need to paint her. He could match her lips if he softened scarlet with a bit of white. Her eyes would be simple; he would just use the same blue as he did for the Virgin's mantle. He wondered if she had golden hair like her brothers. He wasn't sure because she was always wearing a wimple. After a while, he stopped thinking about painting altogether and simply drank her in.

"Isn't it disrespectful to stare at me when it's God you've come to see?"

Alexander jumped as her voice cut through the intense silence. She must have felt his gaze because she hadn't even looked in his direction.

Alexander rushed to defend himself, blurting the first thing that came to his mind, "I don't think God minds when we admire His creatures." His face went scarlet before the words finished escaping.

Ilona let out a surprised laugh and then startled as the sound of her voice echoed around the room. She pressed her lips tightly together in a futile attempt to contain her amusement.

Alexander opened his mouth hoping he could produce words that would save him. "Oh… I am sorry, Your Highness… my um, Kaltic isn't very good."

"Your Kaltic is perfect," she laughed, "better than that of most Kalts. You have a gift for language, you know."

Alexander begged God to smite him right then and there. When a moment passed and he hadn't been incinerated, he fled the room.

He flew back to his chamber, and slammed the door behind him. He stood, trembling head to foot, rebuking himself for his stupidity. *Why did he say that? Why on Earth did he say that?* His mind was immediately flooded with alternative responses. Any of them would have been better than what he said.

What made the whole thing worse was that he shouldn't have been staring at her in the first place. It was disrespectful and he was supposed to be praying. That's when Alexander was hit with an awful realization.

He was in love.

Hopelessly smitten. Ilona was beautiful in mind, body, and soul. He never felt so at home with anyone, and the idea of leaving her was torture.

But what else could he do? He was a candle maker and she was a princess.

He was suddenly swept to a reality where he was still a king. He took her home to Kalathea and laid the whole kingdom at her feet. He offered her a sun that shone all winter and a turquoise sea that glimmered in its light. A palace three times the size of Erkscrim, a library it would take her whole lifetime to read. He would offer her silks and spices from the East, and camels and elephants and one of those long-necked, orange and brown spotted goat things they used to get from Ethiopia.

She would be amazed by it all. He would take her in his arms and kiss her perfect lips and—

He snapped himself from his fantasy. It was just a fantasy. His feelings were an insult and the most loving thing he could do would be to purge them from his heart. He begged God to free him from his desire, but his passion remained.

The only thing he could do was avoid her entirely.

The following day, Alexander hid in his room. Shortly before the noon bell rang, hunger compelled him to slip out. To his horror, Ilona spotted him in the halls.

"Alexander!" she called.

He quickened his pace, pretending not to hear her.

"Alexander!" she repeated, catching him by the shoulder.

"Princess," he answered, turning toward her and bowing respectfully.

"Where have you been?" she asked.

He furrowed his brow and looked as confused as he possibly could.

"My, um, Kaltic," he began. "Please speak more slowly."

Ilona rolled her eyes. "Are you embarrassed, Alexander?"

"Embarrassed?" Alexander repeated, looking more confused than ever. "I don't know that word."

She scowled at him, "Stop it."

"Stop what?" he asked.

"Your Kaltic has been flawless up until now."

"Ah," Alexander answered. "But I am unwell, and I... lose the words..." He knew he was being ridiculous, but for reasons that were beyond him, he kept going. "I... um... *forget.*"

Then, Ilona said something he couldn't understand. When his only response was a blank stare, she repeated the phrase more slowly.

"*We speak a few Greek,*" Ilona answered in Greek. "*How do we saying to speak like so?*"

For a moment, Alexander forgot his humiliation and he twisted his lips as he tried to conceal a smile.

"*So you speak my tongue better than I am spoken to your tongue?*" Ilona continued.

A laugh escaped him. "You speak Greek better than any Kalt I've known," Alexander answered in perfect Kaltic.

"And you speak Kaltic better than any Kalt I've ever known," Ilona answered in her native tongue.

Alexander smiled. He was impressed that she knew as much Greek as she did. He wondered when she learned, and why she learned. He was about to ask her when he remembered that he was avoiding her.

"Forgive me," he said, giving her a little bow. "I have to go."

She looked confused but nodded. "Will I see you later?"

He wished she had just punched him in the nose. "Maybe at supper?" he answered and then scurried away before she could say anything else.

He did not come to supper that evening. For the next week, Alexander spent most of his time hiding in his room. Occasionally, he encountered Ilona in the halls, and then he kept their conversations brief. It tore him apart. It didn't help that Ilona kept trying to find him. She noticed his aloofness, but no inquiry on her part could produce the reason.

One evening, as Alexander sat in his room with his nose buried in a book, he heard a familiar voice.

"You're hurting her, My King."

Alexander looked up to see Brother Joseph standing by the door. He sighed. He was getting tired of the fairies appearing wherever and whenever they wanted without warning. He glared over the top of his book at the old man.

"I don't know what you're talking about," he grumbled, though he knew exactly what Joseph was talking about. "And stop calling me 'My King.'"

"If you feel like distancing yourself is the right course of action, then do it. But tell her why first," Brother Joseph said.

Alexander turned red and hid his face deeper in his book. "I can't. It would humiliate her."

"Her?" Brother Joseph asked with a hint of a smile.

"But supposing she isn't ashamed?" Alexander let the book fall into his lap and looked at Joseph wide-eyed. "Supposing she returns my affections?"

"Supposing?" The old monk laughed. "Are you completely blind?"

"That would make our parting all the more painful," Alexander continued. "Either way it will be painful."

"With all due respect, My King," Brother Joseph replied. "If you are unwilling to feel pain, you are incapable of love."

11

Upholding Kaltic Honor

Brother Joseph was right of course. He was always right. (Not that Alexander resented his rightness. He just brooded about it sometimes.)

Alexander sent the princess a note asking if they could meet in the garden. Waiting for her to arrive was worse than waiting for execution. He paced back and forth wringing his hands until he saw her approaching. She greeted him with a warm smile.

Alexander bowed to her. "Princess, thank you for meeting me here. I… um…."

He'd rehearsed it countless times in his head, but it wasn't coming out anything like he imagined.

"I feel like I… I wanted to explain why I've been so cold," he said finally.

He realized that his hands were shaking. He kneaded them together in an attempt to calm his nerves. It was a failed attempt.

Ilona's pleasant smile broadened slightly.

"I don't want you to think I don't like you; on the contrary, I think you are lovely, very lovely, the loveliest person I've ever met," he said but he was turning red and starting to shrink. "I um… I think I… I know I…" here it came, the death blow. "I am in love with you."

She was grinning ear to ear, but Alexander didn't seem to notice, he quickly added, "I don't expect you to return my affections, I know I am not worthy of a princess."

"Ooooooooooohhhhh," she replied. "That's what you've been worried about." She rolled her eyes and shook her head. "For heaven's sake, Alexander! You're so dramatic." She started walking back toward the keep and gestured for him to follow. She was chuckling. "I really wish you'd told me that earlier!"

Alexander was feeling lost. He imagined several possible reactions, some involved anger, some involved tears, and most involved scoffing. He was completely unprepared for whatever it was she was doing.

She threw open the doors to the great hall and stormed in. The kings were sitting around a table with their knights and nobles. Everyone looked at the princess as she entered.

"My dear brothers!" she called. "There is a matter that is weighing heavy on my heart!"

"What is it, sister?" Florian replied.

"Alexander the Greek is leaving in the morning and we haven't properly thanked him for the service he's rendered to our family," she said.

Alexander finally caught up to Ilona and bowed to the kings.

"You're right!" Filbert said. "He saved our lives!"

"Yes," Added Florian. "Saved us from ourselves! That was no small feat."

"I want you to swear before Alexander, before me, before God, and," Ilona gestured broadly across the room, "before all the good men assembled here, that you will give him anything he asks for."

"We swear it," agreed the kings.

"Really? Even if he asks for all the gold in Kaltehafen?"

"He shall have it!" Florian exclaimed and all the room cheered in agreement.

"What if he asks for the heads of all his enemies?"

"Then we shall hunt them down!" Filbert exclaimed, and all the room cheered in agreement.

76

She looked at Alexander with a mischievous smile and cried. "What if he asks you for the hand of the princess in marriage?"

"He shall have—" Filbert started then stopped himself. "Wait a moment; you're our baby sister, not some prize!"

Ilona looked at her brother horrified. "You just swore before your entire court that you would give him ANYTHING!"

"Yes, but, that was hyperbole!" Filbert continued. Florian was looking back and forth between Ilona and Alexander with a knowing smile. He swatted his brother on the back of his head.

"I, at least, am a man of honor!" he declared. "And even if he asked for what is most precious to me, I would gladly give it."

The people cheered once again.

"But!" Filbert began.

"Brother," Ilona answered Filbert. "I am ashamed of you. What kind of king doesn't keep his promises? But we are getting ahead of ourselves, why not let him speak for himself?"

"Yes, Alexander," Florian agreed. "How can we reward you for your service?"

When the attention in the room went to Alexander, Florian whispered something into Filbert's ear. Filbert glanced back and forth between Alexander and Ilona, a glimmer of realization entering his eyes.

Alexander had his hands folded in front of his lips thoughtfully. He was concealing a smile, his face was scarlet. Then, for the first time in his life, he spoke boldly before the royal court, "For the service I have rendered your family, I will accept nothing less than the hand of the princess. I cannot think of anything you could offer me that I would treasure more than that."

Ilona was struggling to keep a straight face, and even Alexander couldn't hide his amusement.

"So be it!" Florian cried. He looked at Ilona. "I am so sorry, sister. It's for the good of the kingdom, you know."

"I know my duty, brother," she replied. "And if marrying this handsome, cordial, Greek is what I have to do to uphold Kaltehafen's honor, that is a sacrifice I am willing to make!"

She ran to Alexander's side and then turned back toward her brothers. "You promise you won't fight at our wedding feast?"

The two kings swore that they would be on their best behavior, which made the court cheer all the more. Alexander and Ilona ran from the hall, hand in hand. As soon as they passed through the doors, they dissolved into a fit of hysterical laughter.

"I suppose this means you love me too?" Alexander asked when he'd finally caught his breath.

She threw her arms around his neck and kissed him. "What do you think?"

Alexander was in a giddy daze when he returned to his room that evening. When he closed the door behind him, he leaned back against it allowing the happiness to consume him.

"Congratulations, My King," came Brother Joseph's voice. "I've never seen you look happier! Actually, I've never seen you look happy at all. It suits you."

"Thank you," Alexander answered, too much in a daze to be annoyed with the old monk's random appearance.

"How does it feel to be engaged to the kings?"

"What are you talking about?" Alexander asked, with an amused half smile.

"When you marry someone, you marry their family too, you know. Love them or hate them, Filbert and Florian are now part of your life."

"They're not so bad," Alexander answered.

"Don't you think Ilona should know what she's getting?"

Alexander's giddiness subsided. "I don't have any family."

"Telling yourself that over and over doesn't make it true," Brother Joseph commented.

Alexander was silent.

"And what happens when a diplomat from the Kalathean court comes to visit Kaltehafen and recognizes you? How will that impact Ilona?" Brother Joseph was going on.

Alexander wrung his hands thoughtfully.

Brother Joseph reached around him to open the door. Then he took Alexander by the shoulders, turned him around, and pushed him out.

"Now, I don't want to see you back in here, until you've told your new family the whole truth." Brother Joseph started to close the door but stopped when he saw the terror in Alexander's eyes. "I wouldn't worry too much, My King. Things seem to work out well for you when you're straightforward with the princess."

12

The Truth Revealed

gain, Alexander was frustrated with the old monk, but he knew he was right. He wondered if this would change anything, or if Ilona would even believe him.

He arranged to speak with her in the garden. It was a warm day. The last of the snow had finally gone, leaving muddy puddles in its wake.

Alexander noticed someone approaching. He stared a long moment—it was undoubtedly Ilona. The warm weather must have compelled her to unveil her hair. She was wearing it braided up beneath a simple circlet.

She greeted him with a warm smile. He returned it.

"You look different today," he observed.

"Do you still want to marry me?" she teased as she sat down beside him.

"I'll consider it. Though I never would have asked to marry you, if I'd known you had such lovely hair."

He took her hands. It was a wonderful feeling, her hands in his. He was no longer confused or questioning the feelings it gave him. For a moment, he considered changing the nature of the conversation they were about to have. For the first time in his life, things were wonderful and the truth could ruin everything. But the insistent tugging on his conscience forced him to proceed.

He opened his mouth to speak and then closed it. He didn't know where to start.

"Ilona," he began. "There is something, actually a lot, you don't know about me."

"I'm intrigued," Ilona replied with an eager smile.

For some reason, this made Alexander even more nervous.

"I am not a candle maker," he stated. "Well, that's not completely true; I am a candle maker now, but I wasn't always." He was stumbling over his words. Why was this so difficult? Why couldn't he just say what he meant? He decided to try another approach.

"What do you know about the Kalathean queen?" he asked.

Ilona thought for a moment. "Not much; her father was one of the Basils I think."

"Do you remember King Alexander?" Alexander asked.

"Who?"

"Right after Basil and before Fausta, there was another king, King Alexander," he said.

"There was?" Ilona questioned. "I don't remember that."

"He only ruled for a short time, before his sister launched a coup and banished him," he went on.

"That's awful," Ilona observed. "Awful planning. He could gather the support of foreign rulers and come back to take revenge. She really should have killed him or at least cut off his nose or his—"

"You terrify me sometimes," Alexander interrupted.

"Tell me," Ilona continued, a knowing glimmer in her eyes. "Did this banished king go to Kaltehafen?"

Alexander felt himself freeze. He nodded nervously.

"And did he get engaged to the Kaltic princess with the hopes of forming an alliance so he could return to Kalathea with an army and get revenge?"

"No!" Alexander interjected. "He got engaged to the Kaltic princess because he'd never met a person so admirable and he longed to spend his life in her company."

She smiled playfully. "Yours are a curious people, Alexander—awful at launching coups and taking vengeance." She leaned in and touched her forehead to his. "I think you'll make an excellent husband though."

"You believe me?" Alexander questioned.

Ilona looked puzzled. "Why wouldn't I?"

"It's a lot to believe," he replied.

Ilona thought for a moment and then shook her head. "No, it actually explains a lot."

Alexander felt a wave of relief wash over him. He proceeded to tell her everything. Every detail of his life in Kalathea, of becoming king, of Fausta's betrayal, his escape, the fairies that helped him along the way—he left nothing out. As the words rolled from his lips, he felt as if shackles were dropping from his limbs. He was so caught up in the liberating feeling he didn't notice Ilona scowling until he completed his story.

He stiffened. Perhaps, he told her too much too soon?

"I am so sorry, I didn't tell you all of this before," he pleaded. "I understand if—"

"You mean to tell me," she interrupted. "That your fairy godmother let you endure years of abuse from your siblings before she decided to help you?"

"I am sure she had a good reason," Alexander explained. "Apparently they exist to teach people virtue, maybe—"

"Well, I'd like to teach her a thing or two about virtue!" Ilona snapped, pounding her fist into the palm of her hand. "I suppose we should tell my brothers about this."

"Do you think they'll be upset?" Alexander asked.

Ilona laughed. "On the contrary, they will be delighted that I'm marrying a king!"

"Former king," Alexander corrected.

Ilona asked her brothers to meet them privately that evening. Filbert and Florian were enraged when they heard about the injustice Alexander suffered at the hands of his people.

"That's deplorable!" Filbert cried.

"Completely!" Florian agreed. "You're our brother now, your enemies are our enemies!"

"Exactly!" Filbert exclaimed. "I say we march on Kalathea at once! We'll raze the city, burn their crops, and sow salt in the earth so that—"

"Can you *not* do those things?" Alexander petitioned.

"What would you have us do?" Florian asked.

"Nothing at all," Alexander answered. "Not that I don't appreciate your generosity, but I have many fond memories of Kalathea and I'd rather you didn't destroy it. Besides, it's not as if every man, woman, and child conspired against me."

"Alright, so we'll conquer Kalathea," Filbert suggested. "Then you can have it back in one piece."

"Thank you," Alexander answered. "But I have no desire to rule over a people that don't want me." Filbert and Florian exchanged a confused glance. "I'd actually rather no one knows about me. I only thought I should tell you in case someone from home learns I'm here. I don't want to make diplomacy… difficult."

The twins were thoroughly perplexed by Alexander's reluctance and continued trying to get him to change his mind. At last, they agreed to respect his decision, though they still didn't understand it.

Alexander went to bed that evening feeling something he'd never felt before—content. Neither guilt, nor worry, nor anxiety harassed him. He had almost forgotten what it was like to live without these feelings tormenting him. He basked in his happiness and allowed it to touch every part of him.

Filbert and Florian were pushy, overbearing, and treated him like a naive little child. They'd also made it abundantly clear that they would do anything to protect him, whether he liked it or not. As elder brothers went, they were perfect. They were family. And despite all their faults, he was happy to have them.

Alexander was so content, he didn't notice Lanzo entering. The dog bounded on to his diaphragm and knocked the wind out of him. The animal was unaware of his own size, and didn't see any issue with his actions.

Normally, Alexander would have pushed him out and secured the door. Instead, he merely adjusted himself so he could breathe, and started petting the dog's head. He looked into those woeful eyes and said: "You're a vile creature and you really need to learn your place." This only made Lanzo's tail thump with violent happiness.

13

Angels Can't Dance

The wedding day came in the blink of an eye. When Alexander and Ilona left the chapel, arm in arm, they found Brother Joseph waiting for them just outside the doors.

Alexander was about to greet him, when Ilona called out: "You cunning devil!"

She broke away from Alexander and gave the old man a gentle punch in the shoulder.

"What have I done to deserve such a greeting?" he asked.

"Don't pretend you weren't planning this," she accused motioning from herself to Alexander and back again.

"Planning what?" he replied, looking exceptionally pleased with himself.

"And why didn't you ever tell me you weren't human?" she demanded.

"Why did you presume I was human?" his tone was slightly offended, but amusement shimmered in his eyes.

Ilona threw her arms around him and hugged him so tight, it looked like she was going to snap the frail man in two.

The rest of the celebration was uneventful, until Filbert had an epiphany. (He claimed he was enlightened by the Holy Spirit, but it was more likely alcohol.) He stated that an infinite number of angels can dance on the head of a pin because angels do not take up space. Florian, similarly enlightened, countered by saying angels can't dance at all because they do not have bodies. The argument escalated, but Alexander was too busy staring wistfully into Ilona's eyes to notice and intervene.

Then, the archbishop overheard the argument, and explained that angels are able to manipulate matter and take the form of humans as Raphael did in the Old Testament, and therefore, they are able to dance. Then, every knight, clergyman, and noble present gave their opinion. Until finally, Filbert punched Florian in the nose, and Florian threw Filbert over the table, and the archbishop hit Florian over the head with a serving platter, and a brawl broke out, which resulted in a bloodied tangle of amateur philosophers and theologians, the likes of which the world had never seen. But by that time, Alexander and Ilona had gone to bed, leaving the kingdom to its fate.

The incident was documented in an ecclesiastical history and was revisited in songs for years afterward. Filbert and Florian loved hearing the event recounted because neither of them could actually remember it themselves.

To Alexander, his wedding was the start of the happiest year of his life. Painting became his primary occupation and soon every church in Kaltehafen and all the surrounding kingdoms were decorated with his artwork. In his spare time, he was with Ilona in the library. He wanted nothing, except maybe children, and he was sure they would come in God's time. He had all the privileges of royalty without any of the responsibilities. It was paradise.

Then one night, Alexander had a dream.

He saw his father standing at the foot of his bed.

"There you are, Alexander! I've been looking everywhere for you! What are you doing in Kaltehafen?" His father noticed Ilona asleep beside Alexander. "Wait a moment. Did you marry a Kaltic girl?"

Alexander threw the blanket over her head to hide her golden hair.

"No," he answered.

"Oh, well if you had, I would have complimented you on your diplomacy," his father replied.

"Why are you here, Father?" Alexander asked. "I thought you were dead."

"And I thought you were in Kalathea," his father replied.

"The Kalatheans didn't want me," Alexander answered. "So, I made a wonderful life for myself here."

His father grimaced. "Really? In Kaltehafen?"

"Yes, Father," Alexander scowled.

"You need to go home, Alexander. Your people are in danger. Your sister is in danger," his father said.

"What kind of danger?"

But Alexander awoke before his father could specify.

He tried to dismiss the dream, but the more he ignored it, the more he felt a tugging on his heart, a persistent feeling that Kaltehafen was not where he was meant to be.

14

Kalathea is Probably Fine

"Let's play a little game," Acacia said, a sinister smile curling on her lips.

She was in one of Kalathea's old amphitheaters, looking out over the arena. The place was packed with spectators, all looking at her with eyes full of both horror and anticipation.

Fausta stood just beside Acacia. No one could see or hear her except the twins and they ignored her. Standing unseen in plain sight was unnerving. Time and again she had tried to call out to the humans around her. She was unable to touch them. She tried knocking over a water jar to get someone's attention, but it wouldn't budge. Everything she touched was fixed in place, impossible to move. The way people looked right through her made her feel like a ghost. She couldn't do anything the twins didn't want her to do. And in that moment, they only wanted her to watch.

Beside Acacia stood one of the kingdom's most respected senators. Fausta had never witnessed such fear in his eyes. Jace stood just behind his sister, biting his lip to contain his giddiness.

Below, circling the arena, snarling, and growling, was a pride of lions. The creatures were the victims of cruelty—scarred and bruised and emaciated. They fought among themselves, their desperation for nourishment turning them against each other.

"Look there," said Acacia, placing one hand on the senator's shoulder and pointing with the other to two iron gates that opened onto the arena. "Behind the first door are five villagers. I haven't seen them myself. They might be elders or children… who knows? Behind the second is a lovely young lady—intelligent, beautiful, and looking forward to a bright future. Oh yes, she's also your daughter."

Acacia's grin broadened when she saw the color drain from the man's face. "Tell me, Senator Clement, which gate should we open?"

"Neither," was his barely audible reply.

"If you don't choose we'll open both," Acacia sneered. "And you'll have the blood of all six victims on your hands."

Jace walked up behind the man and whispered. "Do you know what's wonderful about this, senator? If you choose your daughter, the people will hate you for killing the villagers. But if you choose the villagers, we'll tell everyone that you sacrificed your daughter to win their votes!" He smiled gleefully. "There's no good outcome for you, I'm afraid. Maybe you'll think twice before opposing us in the future?"

Fausta felt anger burning through her. Watching these beings abuse her people was torture.

"Where is the queen?" the senator demanded. "I want to speak with her immediately."

Acacia glanced at Fausta. A hint of a smile touched her lips. Fausta was using every ounce of willpower to keep herself from crying out to him. She knew it was futile and didn't want to give her captors the satisfaction of seeing her react.

"Why does everyone keep asking that?" Acacia laughed.

"It really is an irrelevant question," Jace added. "Why would you need a queen when your gods have returned?"

This was only the most recent of the twin's cruel games. They regularly gathered the people to witness such events. Each one involved a complex moral dilemma illustrated with the lives of random citizens.

If Fausta had been paying attention, she might have noticed that the new gods never killed anyone themselves. Certainly, they would threaten those who opposed them. Lightning would strike the ground immediately beside the person in question… sometimes the Earth would shake, sometimes fire would surround the victim, but each time someone was actually executed, it was a human agent that carried out the order.

Not a soul among the Kalatheans knew that fairies couldn't kill humans without killing themselves. Few mortals did. One of those mortals was in Kaltehafen, trying desperately to distract himself from the awful feeling that was nipping at his heart.

Jt was only a dream. That's what Alexander told himself whenever he thought back to his father's visit. After he awoke, he asked everyone if they had any news of Kalathea. He asked Florian, the friars, the merchants he knew from his time as a candle maker, but no one could tell him anything.

So he tried to push the matter out of his mind, and returned to his usual routine. The demand for his artwork was growing so that he could hardly keep up with his commissions. He converted an old storage building near the stables into a workshop. There, he spent most of his time. It was luxurious compared to his home in the swamp, though he did have to snatch invasive poultry once in a while and toss them out the window.

Ilona was usually out during the day, overseeing the construction of her cathedral. Occasionally, she would spend her day writing letters requesting the support of artists, theologians, and clergymen. She did this from Alexander's workshop, simply for the opportunity to spend time with him.

On one such day, as they were each quietly engrossed in their work, Florian entered. Alexander tensed when he felt the king looking over his shoulder.

"What are you painting?" he asked.

"Theotokos," Alexander answered.

Florian scrutinized the image, tilting his head back and forth to better perceive its unfinished form.

"Why does St. Theotokos look just like God's mother?" he questioned.

Alexander died a little inside.

"Because that's *literally* what Theotokos means," Ilona answered.

"Oh," Florian answered. "I didn't know that."

"Everyone knows that, Florian," Ilona explained (and in medieval Kaltehafen, it was generally true).

Alexander turned to face him. "Is there something I can do for you, My King?"

"You can give me back my dog," Florian stated. "I need him for a hunt."

Alexander pointed to a bench along the wall under which Lanzo was sleeping. "I'll thank you to remove him; I've been trying all morning."

Florian clapped. "Lanzo! Up!"

The old dog opened his eyes, looked over at Florian lazily, and then went back to sleep.

Florian gave the animal several more insistent orders, all of which he ignored. The king had to pull him out by the scruff of his neck, and throw him over his shoulder. The old dog whined a little, but offered no other resistance.

Lanzo was not a small dog and Florian holding him like so was a testament to his strength.

"You really expect that animal to hunt?" Ilona asked skeptically.

"He is my best hunting dog!" Florian insisted.

"Was," Ilona corrected. "He's little more than a pelt now."

Alexander smiled at this; he loved her brutal honesty when it wasn't directed at him.

"Watch your tongue," Florian replied. "Not one of my knights is as loyal as Lanzo."

"I hope you won't have such difficulty waking them next time we are under attack," Ilona answered.

Florian glared at her, but decided not to engage further. Ilona responded with a satisfied smile as he turned to leave.

"Your Majesty," Alexander called.

Florian turned back to face him.

"Have you heard any news at all from Kalathea recently?"

"Would you like me to send someone there for you?" Florian asked.

Alexander shook his head. "I wouldn't want to burden anyone with such a long journey."

"It would be better than burdening me with your constant inquiries."

Florian must have noticed the concern in Alexander's eyes because he softened a bit, and then added. "I promise if I hear anything I will inform you immediately."

"Thank you," Alexander replied, turning back to his work. Again, he felt Florian scrutinizing his painting.

"Why are her eyes so big?" the king asked.

"Because she is in the presence of God," Alexander explained. "It's symbolic."

"I don't like it, you should make it realistic," Florian commented. "Also, you should make her blonde. God's mother would be blonde."

Alexander sighed very deeply, then said: "I'll make you a candle any way you want it; my painting is my own."

15

The Great Schism

Later that afternoon, Alexander and Ilona took a walk around the castle. They spoke about a number of things, progress of the cathedral, books they were reading, the work of this philosopher or that.

As Alexander listened to Ilona, he was struck by her insightfulness, and overwhelmed with joy in thinking that he had married a woman so wise. As he leaned in to kiss her, he said something that sounded romantic in his head, "You have the face of a Kalt, but the heart of a Kalathean."

Instead of a kiss, he received a slap in the face.

"Let me make something clear," Ilona scolded. "This is a *Kaltic* heart, and I've a *Kaltic* mind, and a *Kaltic* soul, and the hand that slapped you was *Kaltic*. If you cannot accept that, why don't you sulk back to your superior kingdom and find a woman worthy of you!"

She stormed off leaving Alexander to wallow in his stupidity. That night, as he lay under the bench in his workshop trying to fall asleep, he spun the incident over in his mind. Maybe it was a stupid thing to say, but Ilona was certainly overreacting.

He rolled over and scratched Lanzo's head. The filthy creature managed to sneak back in. Alexander would have shoved him out and locked the door, except that he was feeling a bit lonely.

As he lay there, quietly brooding, he became aware of a high purring tone like a cat, but… not a cat. He listened again. There was a clucking and the rustling of feathers and then another purr.

He swore to himself. He must have left the window open. He peered out from under the bench and saw a line of chickens huddled on a beam above. He was too frustrated and too exhausted to chase them out. How he longed for civilization! Where people and dogs and chickens all knew their place.

He spun fond memories of his homeland over and over in his mind, until his eyes grew heavy and he drifted off to sleep.

"Alexander?" someone said.

He opened his eyes to see a pair of feet standing in front of his bench. Their owner leaned down to look at him. It was his father.

"Alexander, what are you doing under there?" he asked.

"I don't want to talk about it," Alexander grumbled.

"When I couldn't find you in your room, I thought you'd returned to Kalathea," his father said.

"I did mention that the Kalatheans hate me, didn't I?" Alexander snapped.

"Looks like you aren't doing any better with the Kalts," his father observed.

Alexander pulled the drop cloth he was using for a blanket over his face. "I should have joined a monastery," he mumbled.

"So do it," his father answered. "And when you encounter difficulties in the monastery, flee to France and hide under another bench."

Alexander didn't mean it of course. He loved Ilona and figured if he avoided her long enough, the matter would resolve itself. He attempted to apply the same logic to his father, and rolled sideways so he was facing the wall. He wasn't in the mood for a lecture at the moment.

"Your people are suffering, Alexander. Are you going to return to Kalathea or will you turn your back on them too?"

Alexander suddenly felt a flicker of anger.

"Like you turned your back on me?" he snapped. He was alarmed at his own boldness. "Whenever Justin was drunk?"

Alexander instantly regretted his outburst when he saw his father's deeply wounded expression.

"Be a better man than I was," his father replied.

Alexander was relieved to find the entire thing had been a dream. Unfortunately, his troubles with Ilona weren't. He spent the next several days sleeping in the same spot until one evening, Florian happened upon him.

"Is she still angry with you?" he asked, leaning over so he could see Alexander under the bench that sheltered him.

Alexander responded by grumbling something indiscernible.

"I can't believe you are letting this continue," Florian exclaimed. "You're her husband aren't you? And that is your bed she banished you from, isn't it?"

Alexander glared sideways at Florian. Technically, it was her bed. After the wedding, she let him sleep in it.

"So be a man! Return to your room, march right up to her, fall on your knees, and beg for mercy!" Florian said.

Alexander grumbled something else inaudible, but in the end, he took Florian's advice. He left his workshop and ventured up the winding stairs to Ilona's chamber. He stood outside the door for a long time, trying to work up his courage. He knocked. There was no response. He knew she was there; he'd seen her go up earlier that evening. He took a breath and entered.

She was standing on the opposite side of the room with her back to him. He could tell her arms were crossed.

"Ilona?"

She turned to face him, scowling.

"I am sorry," he started. "I want to make this right. It's um… a bit lonely down there."

"You have the dog," Ilona stated. "Which I am sure is preferable to a Kaltic woman."

Alexander felt a flash of anger. "That was uncalled for," he asserted. "Do you think I would have married you if I hated Kalts?"

"But I am not a Kalt," Ilona sneered. "I am a golden-haired Kalathean."

"It was a slip of the tongue, Ilona! Sometimes, sometimes, I just… say things."

Her expression softened slightly.

"I didn't mean it," he continued, relaxing slightly. "I-I do it all the time. So there's really no reason to get emotional."

All progress was instantly lost. A fire raged in Ilona's eyes.

"Oh but you *did* mean it!" she hissed. "You're always thinking it, aren't you?"

"Thinking what?"

"About how superior you are!"

Alexander was stupefied. He had no idea where she was getting that idea.

"I am not!" Alexander objected.

"Then why are you always correcting me?" she asked.

"What are you talking about?" he pleaded.

"When we're in chapel, you're always correcting my Latin," she complained.

"I did it once," Alexander scoffed.

"You do it *every time*!" Ilona insisted.

"Do I?"

"Yes! Do you have any idea how irritating that is?" she was going on.

"There are just a few words you struggle—"

"Why do you care?" Ilona exclaimed. "When you say we shouldn't be using Latin in the first place?"

"If you insist on using it," Alexander stated. "You should at least use it correctly."

"And you called the Pope an infidel."

"I thought we agreed never to talk about the Pope," Alexander reminded.

"We did!" Ilona affirmed. "And then you called him an infidel."

"When was this?"

"Last month, when my uncle was visiting," she said.

"Oh for heaven's sake, your uncle started that. He's always talking politics and—"

"THE POINT IS," Ilona interrupted. "You're always going on about how in Kalathea you do things this way or that way and whatever way it is, is better than how we do it here!"

"What does that mean?"

"You wish you could go home, don't you? Leave us savages and go back to the civilized world!" she snapped.

Alexander was silent. He mulled over her words.

"Ilona, please listen. Because you are right about something. I do miss home. Miss it terribly. I miss seeing people who look like me, I miss speaking in my own tongue. But Ilona…" he sighed. "You are so stubborn, so, so… *incredulous*… how could you think for a moment that I'd ever want to leave you behind?"

"Because you wish you'd married someone more civilized," she said.

"No. I don't." Alexander snapped. "And even if I had to forget about Kalathea and spend the rest of my days in this… in this…"

"In this *what*?" Ilona dared.

"In Kaltehafen," Alexander dodged. "I would do it for you."

Ilona regarded him for a long moment. Her silence frightened him.

"I love you," he added, hoping it would shield him from whatever was coming next.

"I am trying to decide whether to kiss you or slap you," she explained.

"May I make a suggestion?" Alexander offered.

The corner of Ilona's lip turned upward slightly, and when he leaned in to kiss her she didn't resist.

"I'm sorry," he repeated. "I never meant to hurt you."

Ilona opened her mouth to speak and then closed it. She was battling with herself about whether or not to say something. He could tell by the way she kept curling her lips.

"I'm sorry, too!" she forced.

Alexander raised his eyebrows. He wasn't expecting that. Before he had time to recover from the shock, she grabbed him by the collar and pulled him into another kiss. Then, he wrapped his arms around her, and as they were holding each other she said, "It wasn't just you, Alex. I shouldn't have snapped at you like that. I suppose I am a bit jealous."

"Jealous? Why?"

"You miss your home, but I'd give anything to leave mine—to be with people who don't look like me, or talk like me, or think like me. That sounds exciting! Escaping the cloister was hard enough; my brothers never let me go anywhere! Believe me; I've tried escaping many, many, times."

"Why didn't you tell me that?" he pressed. "We can go somewhere."

"Where?" she asked.

He kissed her again. "Anyplace you like!"

"Kalathea?" she teased.

"Except Kalathea," he smiled.

Then, they spent hours talking about the places they'd like to visit and when they could make their escape, until they grew tired of talking and decided to occupy their time in other ways. Thus, the schism in their marriage was healed. (Unfortunately, they were not able to resolve the schism in the larger church that evening, but I digress.)

The entire matter was forgotten and happiness returned to Erkscrim.

For a little while.

16

Eda Drops In

Alexander sat in the great hall staring vacantly at his uneaten food. He was trying to listen to Ilona, who was still listing the places she wanted to visit. Unfortunately, despite his best efforts, his mind kept returning to his dreams and to Kalathea.

"Alex?" Ilona asked, pulling him from his thoughts. She must have realized he wasn't listening.

"Sorry," he replied.

"Are you thinking about your father again?" Ilona whispered.

"My father?" was Alexander's only response.

"I thought so," she replied. "Do you want to go talk about it?"

"I don't know," Alexander shrugged.

What was left to talk about? How could he act on a feeling he couldn't confirm? And even if he could confirm it, what was he supposed to do?

The last thing he heard about Kalathea was what Eda told him the day she brought him to Kaltehafen. Jace and Acacia were still with his sister, their game unfinished, their next move unclear.

But how was it his concern? The kingdom was no longer his responsibility. As for Fausta, this was all her doing. Anything that happened to her was her own fault.

He hardly even missed Kalathea. Well, he missed a few things, like the turquoise blue of the ocean, the warmth of the summer breeze, the history, the art, the culture, the mild winters, and access to running water. He really, really, really missed running water.

Alexander kept hoping that Brother Joseph would come to see him. Surely, he would have some news and some advice to go along with it. He hadn't seen the old monk since his wedding and had no idea how to contact him. He had disappeared from St. Loudon's. When Alexander asked where he had gone, none of the other monks knew who he was talking about. It was like he had never existed.

He rubbed his forehead. He had an awful headache. It was frustrating to have a feeling that he could neither get rid of nor do anything about. Since he wasn't sure who to be angry with for this dilemma, he chose God by default.

He grumbled a prayer in his mind.

If there's something You want me to do, You might be a bit more straightforward. The least You could do is send someone to help me.

At that very moment, Eda crashed through the ceiling. It was like a giant hand hurled her from the sky straight through the roof and into the ground. Her impact created a crater in the middle of the floor. The entire hall stood looking dumbstruck at the smoking hole and its crumbled occupant.

Ilona leapt over the table and ran toward the crater. Alexander followed cautiously. By the time he reached the perimeter of the newly formed pit, Ilona was already kneeling beside Eda.

Eda looked like an Amazon warrior with her ancient armor and the sword clutched in her hand. She lay with her eyes closed, battered and bloody. Alexander had never seen her look so... mortal.

"Is she alive?" he mumbled. The idea of a fairy dying shook him to the core.

"I don't know," Ilona started. Then, Eda's eyes shot open and she leapt to her feet. She pointed her blade toward the opening in the roof and cried: "WHY DON'T YOU COME AND FINISH ME! I DARE YOU! WHAT'S IT TO YOU IF WE CRUSH THESE PUNY MORTALS?"

When she received no reply, she let out a maniacal laugh that put villains everywhere to shame.

"AS I THOUGHT, COWARD!"

She looked around the room at the dumbstruck spectators and declared, "I am Eda, the Fairy of War and I—"

"Wait a moment," Alexander interrupted. "I thought you were the Fairy of Prudence."

"Silence!" Eda snapped. "I will not be reduced to a mere personification! I am the fairy of many things!"

"How dare you speak to—" Ilona began, but Eda cut her off.

"Alexander, is that you?" she asked, squinting.

"Yes?" came Alexander's confused response.

"Ah, good! I have something critically important to tell you about Kalathea!"

"What is it?" he pleaded.

But Eda's eyes closed and she crumpled back down in the crater and lay still. Alexander had no idea what to do, so he had Eda carried to a bed and then sent for a physician.

The physician's prognosis wasn't hopeful.

"She's dead," he declared.

"Are you sure?" Alexander asked, turning white with horror.

"Well she isn't breathing and doesn't have a heartbeat so, yes."

"But she's not human, maybe…"

"I am afraid humans are all I really know," the doctor shrugged. "I suppose you could always leave her out in the sun a couple of days and see if she starts to decay.

Alexander turned green.

"Leave whom, where?" came Eda's voice. She was sitting upright on the bed as though completely refreshed and ready to leave.

"Oh look at that," the doctor marveled. "I suppose you were right."

"Oh, Alexander, you didn't send for a human physician did you?" Eda sighed. She started dabbing her forehead with her fingers and mumbling. "Oh please tell me he didn't drill a hole in my head."

"Don't be absurd," the doctor rebuked. "I'd only do that if blood was pooling in your skull."

"Of course I sent for a doctor, you were... dead," Alexander defended.

"What do you expect a doctor to do for a dead person?" Eda asked.

"That's what I was wondering!" the doctor added.

Alexander opened his mouth to speak but was too confused to think of a reply. Ilona came to his rescue.

"So what *can* we do to help you?" she asked.

"Nothing," Eda answered. "Don't do anything, *please*. I'll heal myself."

"Fine," Ilona answered. "You'll have all the time you need. Now are you going to tell me why you blew a hole in my roof?"

"Excuse me, Your Highness," the doctor interjected. "But may I leave now? This is all completely beyond me."

"Oh, of course," Ilona answered. "Thank you, doctor."

"Ilona, perhaps we should come back later when Eda's had a little more time to heal?" Alexander suggested.

"No!" Ilona protested. "No one smashes a hole in my roof without explaining themselves."

"Come now, Ilona," Alexander petitioned. "Have a little mercy; she was dead a moment ago."

"She looks fine to me," Ilona answered. Then, looking at Eda, she added, "I expect you to answer all of my questions clearly and directly. No riddles. No games. No telling us we have to learn for ourselves."

"I like you," Eda smiled. "Of course I will explain everything, but first, there is something critical I must tell Alexander... what was it...?" She rubbed her forehead thoughtfully.

"Was it about Kalathea?" Alexander asked hopefully.

"Yes!" Eda replied. "That's right! I was going to tell you... Do not go back there under any circumstances!"

"I have the death sentence there," Alexander reminded her. "I wasn't planning to go back."

"Right," Eda remembered. "But there was another reason..."

Alexander wondered what other reason he needed.

She furrowed her brow thinking. "I apologize. This was all so clear to me before I got ambushed..."

"Ambushed?" Alexander exclaimed.

"Yes," Eda answered. "Just a moment..."

"Was it the twins?" he interjected.

Eda laughed, "The twins? Really, Alexander?"

Alexander couldn't see what was so amusing about his question.

"Oh, that's right!" Eda remembered. "We were going to help you take back your kingdom."

"You were?" Alexander asked blankly.

"You might have told him that," Ilona grumbled.

Eda rolled her eyes. "I thought it was obvious. Did you really think we'd make you live in Kaltehafen for the rest of your life?"

"Is there something wrong with Kaltehafen?" Ilona scowled.

"In any case, none of this matters now," Eda sighed. "We've gone to war, Alexander. And—"

"With whom?" Ilona interrupted.

"Just some rebels; it isn't important," Eda dismissed.

"Fairy rebels?" Alexander asked.

"No, gnome rebels," Eda replied, rolling her eyes. "Of course, they are fairies! Who else would we go to war with?"

"That seems important to me," Alexander commented. The idea of two groups of god-like beings throwing each other through buildings struck him as something humanity should know about.

"It's no concern of yours; remember we can't kill humans, even accidentally, without killing ourselves. Why do you think my enemy left me, after I fell through the roof?"

"So you're using us as a shield?" Ilona scolded.

"Absolutely!" Eda replied. "It's not hurting you, is it? And Alexander owes me a favor anyway." She looked at Alexander. "Since this war isn't likely to end in your lifetime, and you can't defeat the twins on your own, you won't be able to reclaim your throne. I'm so sorry, Alexander. You are just going to have to live out your life quietly, beekeeping or painting or whatever it is you do."

Alexander couldn't believe what he was hearing. A fairy telling him to forget about Kalathea and move on with his life. It was exactly the validation he was hoping for. He felt a surge of joy, and then immediately felt guilty, remembering that he was only free because the fairies were at war.

"I suppose the twins have gone away to war also?" Alexander asked hopefully.

Eda laughed. "You think those two would pick a fight with an equal? They're children! They'll stay in Kalathea until they lose interest in Kalathea."

"Oh," Alexander replied, his heart sinking.

"That's why you must never go back, Alexander," Eda insisted. "No matter what you hear."

"What would I hear?" Alexander asked.

"Rumors, news, happenings, anything. Ignore it," Eda answered.

"You have some news, don't you?" Ilona accused.

"It doesn't matter," Eda replied. "You can't do anything about it, so why do you want the burden of knowing?"

"We can *pray*," Ilona replied.

Eda narrowed her eyes suspiciously.

"My sister is in Kalathea," Alexander insisted. "If she is in some kind of danger, don't I have a right to know?"

"Human curiosity is the bane of my existence," Eda sighed. "Fine."

The first thing she told them was that no one had seen Fausta in months. Then, she told them of the twin's sadistic games, and how they had set themselves up as gods over the people.

The news was like a knife in Alexander's heart. His father's words were true, the people were suffering. The news of his sister's disappearance troubled him more than anything. He didn't know why. He told himself over and over again that it was her own fault. It didn't make him feel any better.

17

The Reluctant King

Alexander's brush hovered over a blank panel. At the moment, he couldn't remember who he was supposed to be painting on it. Maybe one of the Apostles? God's mother was always a safe bet.

He set his brush down. It was only a day since Eda's unexpected arrival, and he couldn't concentrate. Eda insisted he let the matter drop, but he couldn't. He picked up his brush and tried again to focus.

"I have an idea!" Ilona proclaimed, bursting into Alexander's workshop. He jumped, dropping his brush into an open paint jar, speckling himself and everything around him.

Florian charged in after her. "Yes! We have an idea!" he repeated.

"About what?" Alexander asked, recovering his brush.

"About saving the Kalatheans!" Ilona exclaimed. "I've been thinking about it a lot and it occurred to me that if fairies are unable to kill humans themselves, then they are only as powerful as their human agents—."

"Take a breath, Ilona," Alexander interrupted. "You're turning blue."

Ilona breathed deeply, and then continued speaking at her previous rate.

"So all we have to do is inform the people of this weakness, and then they won't have to follow the twins anymore. They will be free!"

"By human agents, you mean the entire Kalathean army," Alexander pointed out. "A powerful force."

"Not as powerful as the Kaltic army!" Florian added gleefully.

"Exactly!" Ilona replied, bouncing up and down with excitement. "Which is why, my brothers are going to conquer Kalathea, give it back to you, and then you are going to inform the twins that the people will no longer serve them. Problem solved!"

Alexander looked at Ilona with one eyebrow raised and his mouth slightly open.

"First off," Alexander began. "What makes you think the Kaltic army stands a chance against the Kalathean army?"

"Because," Florian replied smugly. "We crushed you in 368, and in 513, and in 782, and just ten years ago Filbert and I sent your brother Justin home to his father in tears."

"You fought my brother?" Alexander asked.

"Who didn't?" Florian answered.

"Fair," Alexander shrugged. "But even if the Kalts could conquer Kalathea, the only thing that could possibly make my people hate me more than they do already is if I lead a barbarian horde against them. No, I think Eda is right."

"Of course I am," Eda answered, materializing right behind Alexander. He jumped, overturning a jar of blue paint. This was the first time Eda had left her room since she crashed in. She didn't look improved. She was battered and pale, and judging by her expression, irritable. Alexander worried that she would drop over dead again. Even if she wasn't actually dead, he didn't want it to happen. It was alarming.

"You cannot fight them," Eda insisted. "They're your superiors in power and intelligence. They may not be able to kill you directly, but oppose them and they will have their vengeance."

"There you have it," Alexander answered, looking for a rag to wipe up the puddle of blue.

"We cannot abandon your people, Alexander," Ilona insisted. "If there is even a small chance that we could be successful, we have to take it!"

"Exactly!" Florian agreed. "We will storm Kalathea and free the people or die trying!"

"How noble of you," Eda commented dryly. "Noble and stupid."

"Is that any way to speak to a king?" Florian snapped.

"Not your preferred way, I'm sure," Eda answered. "But I've said worse to greater kings."

"Why you insolent little—" Florian started and continued with a string of threats and insults that only fed the amusement in Eda's eyes.

As Alexander mopped up the puddle of blue, he listened for Ilona to join the argument. This was usually what happened whenever Florian started ranting. Ilona would intervene, and the situation would escalate, and once they had a good fight, they would calm down and Alexander could lead them in a respectable discussion.

But Ilona didn't say a word. Alexander stood, holding the sopping blue rag in his hand and looked at her curiously.

She was lost in thought.

"...In all my thousand years, I've never heard that word used that way," Eda was saying to Florian. "I admire your creativity."

Before Florian could produce a fresh wave of insults, Ilona spoke.

"I have another idea," she interjected suddenly, and the attention of all turned to her.

Ilona discussed her plan with Alexander late into the evening, adding details and contingencies. He listened mostly, weighing their chances of success in his mind. Just thinking about it made him queasy. Even if her scheme worked and the people abandoned their new gods, there was no guarantee they would accept his kingship. It was almost impossible to convince Florian that he couldn't simply walk into Kalathea and claim the throne.

"Aren't you the son of Basil?" Florian had objected.

"Yes, but that isn't enough," Alexander explained. "The Senate must acknowledge my kingship."

"I've never heard anything so absurd," Florian exclaimed. "Do you always have to answer to the Senate?"

"Yes, no… um… it's complicated," Alexander replied.

"What is the point of being a king if you have to answer to a senate?" Florian ranted. "Why, if I had to answer to a senate, I'd never get anything done!"

But no amount of ranting could change the way of things. Alexander needed time to think. Long after Ilona went to bed, Alexander remained behind, wandering the castle corridors. He was struggling with something, something he hadn't told anyone.

He didn't want to do it.

If he proceeded with the plan, he risked losing everything. And even if they were successful, then he would have to be king again, which was like losing everything anyway.

But the suffering of the people weighed on his heart. He was the last heir of Kalathea; how could he abandon them? Then his mind wandered back to the night of Justin's murder. He remembered how the people swarmed around him and beat him and tore at him and called for his head.

He remembered standing before the Senate, searching the crowd for one kind face and finding none. He remembered how Fausta avoided his every attempt to catch her eye. He never felt so loathed and so alone.

He didn't care if Kalathea burned.

He started back toward his room. In the morning, he would tell Ilona he was going to take Eda's advice and forget the whole thing. He felt a knot in his stomach. She wouldn't like it. He didn't completely like it himself. He tried to ignore his dissatisfaction, but the tugging on his heart grew stronger the closer he came to his room.

It was inescapable, relentless. He became angry.

What do You want me to do? he thought. *None of this is my concern!*

He stormed into his room. He saw a lump of blankets that had once been Ilona. He didn't worry about waking her. Nothing could wake her once she was asleep. He took the knife off his belt and started looking for the little chest where he usually kept it. The chest was always in the same place, and Alexander would have spotted it in an instant if he hadn't been tangled in his thoughts.

What kind of a fool would I have to be to risk my own happiness for the people who tried to kill me?

He found the chest, and tossed his knife in. The sound of it knocking against something pulled Alexander back to reality. He withdrew the second item.

It was Brother Joseph's gift, the worn wooden crucifix. It was then he realized exactly what sort of fool would do something like that.

He clutched it in his hand and sinking to the floor buried his face in his knees. He stopped rationalizing with himself. He knew what he had to do. He'd always known.

In his heart, he accepted his mission. All at once, the tugging ceased and at last he was at peace with himself. No less angry about what happened in his past, no less afraid of what was going to happen in the future, now he had a clear path he was determined to follow no matter what.

18

Eda Rebels

In the weeks afterward, Alexander worked closely with Ilona and Florian to set their plan in motion. He couldn't remember ever seeing the siblings so excited. Their every interaction was filled with lively chatter as if Christmas was coming and they weren't all about to die.

Alexander realized on the off-chance they were successful, that Ilona would need to be fluent in Greek to even have a chance of being accepted as queen. So he started speaking to her exclusively in his own language. He was impressed by how quickly she improved.

There was something else Alexander wanted to do before he left. Whenever Ilona was occupied, he would slip into his workshop. He had promised her, before they were married, that he would complete the altarpiece for her cathedral at some point in his lifetime.

He was becoming increasingly aware that she was giving up everything for him—her home, her language, and her people. He asked if she was at all disappointed about giving her cathedral project over to someone else, to which she replied that she planned to build another one in Kalathea (but it would be slightly shorter).

The least Alexander could do for her was finish her altarpiece. Sitting there quietly focused took his mind off what was to come. He lost himself completely in the biblical scenes as he brought them to life. When he finished each evening, he locked the door so she wouldn't see it. She probably thought he'd forgotten and he wanted to keep it that way until he was finished.

Eda was not happy about any aspect of the plan, and made communicating this her life's mission. She would appear at random during their preparations and try to talk them out of it, saying things like: "Why don't you just fling yourselves off the outer wall? It would be more efficient and less painful."

She was recovering, as far as Alexander could see. He wasn't sure if her visible wounds were real, or if she was just manifesting her injuries in a way that humans could comprehend. Fairies were such a puzzle.

The more she recovered, the more short-tempered and out-of-sorts she became. Alexander wondered if the war was weighing on her mind. He wished he could do something for her, but helping his own kind was challenging enough. He wouldn't have any idea how to start with a fairy.

Late one afternoon, he returned to his room in search of a book. He was hoping to finish it before he marched off to certain death. If things went according to plan, that would be in about a month's time. He found Ilona lying on the bed, sound asleep. He thought it odd that she was asleep so early, and fully clothed, and on top of the covers.

When he approached to check on her, he was alarmed to find her breathing faint and her heart beat so soft and slow he could barely find it at all. He tried desperately to wake her and was about to call for help, when someone spoke.

"She's alright, Alexander. I've just put her in an enchanted sleep."

He looked up to see Eda standing between himself and the door.

"I am about to do the same to you."

"What? Why?" Alexander cried.

"Since you are intent on going to Kalathea with or without my help, I am going to put you to sleep until the war is over. Now, I recommend you lie down; I don't want you to collapse and hit your head on something."

"But what about her brothers? If this war is going to last as long as you think, they'll be dead when we wake. She'll be heartbroken," Alexander said.

"So I'll put them to sleep also," Eda shrugged. "I'll put this whole damn kingdom to sleep if it will make you happy, but you're not going back to Kalathea without me."

She took a step forward and Alexander took a step back. He didn't know why; once she decided to knock him out, it wouldn't matter where in the room he was.

"Wait, please!" Alexander protested. "Isn't this my choice to make?"

"Certainly," Eda replied. "And knocking you out is my choice to make. It's called free will, kid."

"Did the High Council approve this?" Alexander questioned.

Eda laughed. "If I asked them to approve everything I did, I'd never get anything done."

"Would they approve, if they knew?"

Eda's lips tightened.

"What… what about Alika and Brother Joseph? Would they agree to this?"

"They aren't here to offer their opinion," Eda replied.

"So now you're rebelling," Alexander accused. "Just like Jace and Acacia and… whoever it is you're fighting."

"I don't need a mortal lecturing me about the error of my ways," Eda responded flatly. "It's demeaning."

"My people need to know the truth," he insisted.

"The twins will make you pay dearly for revealing it," Eda countered.

"What makes me so important?" Alexander snapped. "Is my life worth more than all the Kalatheans who will die while I am trapped here?"

Eda regarded him silently for a moment. She furrowed her brow. Her eyes became glassy and just a bit red.

"No, Alexander. Your life isn't worth more than theirs. It's just…" She paused, looked up toward the ceiling and blinked until her eyes cleared. "…of all the people I've been assigned…" she sighed. "I like you, Alexander, and I want you to live."

Alexander softened. "Is your purpose to keep me alive or to help me do what's right?"

Eda glared at him but gave no answer. He noticed a tear on her cheek, before she turned her face away.

"To be completely honest," Alexander continued. "I don't want to do this either. I'm terrified. Terrified of dying and even more terrified of living as a king. Everything in me wants to abandon this mission. Please, Eda. I need someone to help me do what's right."

Eda wiped her eye with her wrist and grumbled, "I hate my job."

"If it's any consolation," Alexander answered. "I hate mine too."

The corner of Eda's lip turned up very slightly. "Want to trade? You're a much better fairy than I am."

Alexander returned her smile. "If only!"

"Go kiss your wife," Eda ordered. When she saw Alexander's confused expression, she added, "It will wake her up."

"Oh…" Alexander answered. He wanted to question this, but didn't think it was the appropriate time. Instead, he shrugged and said, "Of course, it will."

He started back for Ilona.

"Oh, Alexander," Eda added. "Don't lose hope. No matter what happens, remember we will be coming for you as soon as we can."

"Thank you," he replied.

Alexander knelt down beside the bed, but as he leaned in to kiss Ilona, he paused and looked up at Eda with a horrified expression.

"How were you planning on waking me up?" he asked.

Eda snickered. "I like you, kid, but not that much. Same way I do any magic, by willing it."

Alexander breathed a sigh of relief.

19

Goodbye, Loathsome Beast

Alexander lay on his back on the grassy lakeshore attempting to dry himself in the sun. His cloak and outer tunic were draped over a nearby tree branch. He had been walking by the water with Ilona a few moments prior, when the urge to go wading overcame him. Ilona, declined to follow him in, so he playfully splashed her. She startled and tumbled into the lake soaking herself completely through.

The moment Alexander pulled her to her feet, she shoved him so that he toppled over completely drenching himself. Then, she refused to let him come to shore until she was satisfied with his pleas for forgiveness.

Luckily for Alexander, his planned departure put Ilona in a forgiving mood. They had an agreement. They would travel to Kalathea separately, stay on the opposite sides of Lysandria, and act as strangers on any chance encounter. Alexander couldn't risk the twins learning of their relationship and taking Ilona hostage.

This was to be their last day together for a long time. They decided to spend it alone, hidden away in the sanctuary of the forest. Ilona lay next to Alexander with her head resting on his shoulder.

"I don't know why I am worried about what will happen in Kalathea when I should be worried about you drowning me here," she grumbled.

"I am so sorry, Ilona," Alexander replied. He had apologized at least seven hundred times since the incident occurred. This made seven-hundred and one. "I feel awful."

"Good," Ilona answered, snuggling into him. "You deserve to feel awful."

For a long moment, they both rested quietly absorbing the sunlight.

"Alexander?" Ilona asked finally.

"Mm hmm?" Alexander replied.

"What is expected of a Kalathean queen?"

"What do you mean?" Alexander replied.

"I mean, do they manage the kingdom's affairs or do they hide away in their chambers weaving tapestries?"

"Some of our queens have lived hidden lives," Alexander explained. "And some have ruled in their own right." He turned his head to look at her. "I have a feeling you will do whatever you please, regardless of tradition."

Ilona grinned. "Of course I will. It is still good to know what's expected of me."

Alexander ran his fingers through her hair. She had been wearing it braided up underneath a thin summer veil, but since her tumble, the veil had been removed and each tangled lock was fleeing in a different direction.

She was sopping and muddy and covered in bits of pond scum. She glared sideways at him when he touched her.

"What are you staring at?" she growled.

"You," he answered with a subtle smile. "Do you have any idea how beautiful you are?"

Ilona scowled.

"Stop trying to save yourself," she advised. "It's pathetic."

"May I kiss you?" he asked.

"Did you hear me?" she retorted, desperately trying to hide a smile.

"What was that?" he responded, leaning in to kiss her. She gave him a little shove, and rolled away, swallowing a giggle.

Alexander looked back toward the sky. Kaltehafen was miserable in the winter but stunning in the summertime. Never had he seen a wood so green or trees so tall. He wanted to lie in that place forever, listening to the orchestra of birdsong that rang all around him. He closed his eyes. He suddenly felt Ilona snuggling back into him.

"Forgive me already?" he asked.

"No, but it's a bit cold over there," she answered.

A long moment passed in which they lay silently, each enjoying the presence of the other.

"Alex, I don't want this day to end," Ilona sighed.

"We'll have more like it," Alexander replied, "when we are home in Kalathea."

A smile touched her lips. "Do you promise?"

"I swear it," he replied. "After our victory, we will slip away and do whatever you like. Name it."

"Then take me to the sea," Ilona answered. "Florian says there's nothing so humbling as standing by the sea. A force that can humble Florian must be something to behold!"

Alexander laughed. "Is that all? You don't need to wait for our victory for that. Turn any corner in Lysandria and you will find yourself on the shore."

"Am I really going?" Ilona asked with a disbelieving smile.

Her excitement delighted him. Kalathea would be a paradise for her, if they could restore it. He was almost afraid he would lose her forever in the library, if she stopped examining the architecture long enough to enter the building.

Of course, even if they were victorious, there would be challenges to overcome. He sighed, thinking of one in particular.

"Ilona, there is something you should know," he paused as he tried to think of the right words. Unfortunately, he couldn't think of any way to make his message less unpleasant. "After our victory, we will need to face the fact that some Kalatheans... actually most Kalatheans... don't really like Kalts."

"Oh, I know," Ilona answered. "Kalatheans are a bunch of pretentious snobs that think they are better than everyone else."

"Wait a moment. You think I am a pretentious snob?" he asked.

Ilona smirked. "Absolutely! But I still love you."

"It isn't that Kalatheans think they are better than Kalts," Alexander corrected. "It is simply that Kalatheans view Kalts as… primitive."

"Do you think that?" Ilona asked.

"*You* are not primitive, Ilona!" Alexander answered. "And I am sure the people will agree, once they get to know you better. I just don't want you to be alarmed if some of the senators call you vile names and then attempt to annul our marriage. That's all."

"What kind of vile names?" Ilona asked.

Alexander shrugged.

"Like insolent, low-born, she-brute?" Ilona suggested.

Alexander blushed. "Maybe something like that."

"Or filthy, barbarian sow?" she tried.

"That wouldn't be beneath them."

Ilona unleashed several more possibilities. Grinning as Alexander became increasingly uncomfortable.

"Don't worry," she finished. "For every insult they hurl my way, I'll reward them with ten."

"Oh dear," Alexander sighed. A picture of a typical day in the Kalathean court was developing in his mind. He consoled himself with a reminder that they wouldn't reach that point for a while yet.

That reminded him that he was leaving in the morning.

"May I kiss you now?" he pressed.

"You're persistent aren't you?" Ilona grinned. She whacked him in the lips with the back of her hand. "You may kiss my hand."

He did so. Then, he kissed the back of her wrist, then her forearm, and started working his way up toward her lips. Ilona tried unsuccessfully to keep a smile from escaping.

"I said, 'my hand,'" she scolded.

"Oh, sorry," Alexander answered. "I must have drifted."

Ilona snorted a laugh and indicated complete forgiveness by grabbing his collar and pulling him in to meet her lips.

The next morning, Alexander loaded a cart full of honey, beeswax, and every item that could be produced from these ingredients—balms, and soaps, and candles. He was to return to Kalathea as a merchant, as per Ilona's instructions.

He was to travel with Florian to the southern half of the Kaltehafen. Filbert would meet them there and continue with their party to Kalathea. Ilona made her brothers promise that they wouldn't leave Alexander's side until the entire affair was over.

Alexander protested, worrying that if their party was attacked all three could be killed off at once leaving both their kingdoms leaderless. (He also didn't like the idea of spending months in close quarters with the Filbert and Florian.) However, Florian insisted that he was going to follow Alexander whether he agreed to it or not.

So on the day of departure, they dressed in the humble attire of Kaltic merchants and prepared to depart. The cart was a significant improvement over the one Alexander owned previously. It was drawn by two horses and there was plenty of room for passengers.

Lanzo trotted after Alexander as he finished making preparations. He was sure the old dog would try to follow him all the way to Kalathea if he didn't restrain him. He looped a rope around its neck, and handed one end to a servant. He knelt down and rubbed the animal between the ears.

"I don't suppose I will see you again," he said. "It's probably for the better. You're a filthy, lazy, beast with neither purpose nor manners."

Alexander felt a weight in his chest as Lanzo started thumping his tail.

"You'd never be allotted this kind of freedom in Kalathea, you know. You'd sleep in the stables where animals belong. Trust me when I tell you, you're better off here."

He tried not to make eye-contact with Lanzo as he stood. He didn't need that kind of guilt burdening him now.

"Maybe you should bring him," Ilona suggested. "If you end up starving in the wilderness, you'll have something to eat."

Alexander scoffed. "Have you looked at this animal? He's old and stringy. Even as rations he's useless. It's a wonder that you keep him around."

"That's just it," Ilona answered. "He's so useless we can't even spare the effort it would take to get rid of him. Now, do you have time left to say goodbye to me, or did you expend it all on the dog?"

"*You* I will see again," Alexander teased. "But I suppose I can spare a little time."

He took her in his arms and held her for so long that Florian had to climb down from the cart and pull them apart. He scolded them and told them that they had been married too long to be so much in love.

Alexander managed to slip the key to his workshop into her hand before boarding the cart. She turned it over in her palm and then shot him a puzzled look.

"See for yourself," he smiled.

She returned his smile, her eyes sparkling with curiosity. "You should go; I want to see what you've made for me."

"Impatient, aren't you?" he smirked.

"Extremely!"

And with that, the cart lurched forward and they were on their way. Alexander waved to Ilona as they moved forward down the road.

"You know, I was in love once," Florian commented bitterly.

"Oh?" Alexander replied watching Ilona as she faded into the distance.

"She's married to Filbert now."

Alexander turned his attention toward Florian. He was feeling deeply uncomfortable, but also unbearably curious.

"She said I wasn't her type," Florian finished, staring wistfully into the distance.

"I see," Alexander mumbled.

What followed was a long and torturous silence. If Alexander had looked sideways at Florian, he may have noticed an amused glimmer in his eye, as if he was basking in Alexander's discomfort. But Alexander was making a conscious effort not to look at him, instead keeping his eyes fixed on the road ahead.

At last, Alexander glanced backward again. He could still see Erkscrim perched among the hills. It occurred to him that he probably wouldn't see the castle again. Certainly, it wasn't much on the eyes, an ugly pile of grey angles jetting up from the hillside. It was freezing in the winter and dark inside even during the day, but it was the place where he spent the happiest days of his life, and for all its flaws, it felt like home.

"I am coming from Kaltehafen. I was born in Lysandria."

The custodian dropped his pen, and looked at Alexander astonished.

"You're a Kalathean?"

"I am, sir," Alexander answered.

"Are you sure you are headed in the right direction?" the official asked.

"Toward home?" Alexander replied. "Where else would I be going?"

"How long have you been gone?"

"Five years."

"Then you've missed some things," the custodian proceeded. "Take my advice; turn around and go right back where you came from."

"It can't be that bad," Alexander answered.

The man grimaced at him.

"If you choose to pass through this gate, you will not be allowed to leave."

"Why not?" Alexander asked.

"The gods have mandated it," the man clarified. "Kalathea is short on Kalatheans."

"Gods?" Alexander replied. "I have missed some things, haven't I?"

"Go home, kid," the custodian grumbled.

"I will if you'll let me," Alexander pressed.

"I mean back to…" he rubbed his forehead with one hand. "Where did you say you were coming from?"

"Kaltehafen."

The custodian let out an irritated sigh and glanced at the twins who were standing behind Alexander. "You aren't the one who's been sending all these Kalts, are you?"

Alexander laughed. "Have many Kalts passed this way?"

"So many, they are all starting to look the same," the man replied, glancing again at Filbert and Florian.

"Perhaps I am!" Alexander answered. "Anyone who heard me boasting of my homeland would migrate immediately!"

The pity the custodian was feeling for Alexander was written plainly on his face.

He shook his head and grumbled: "What do you have in your cart?"

"Every good a bee can provide, honey, beeswax, soap—"

"You were selling soap to the Kalts?" the official questioned. "God bless you."

"Don't you mean gods bless you?" Alexander replied.

The official rolled his eyes, "Whatever."

He walked around to the back of the cart and examined the contents, then lifting out a sealed jug of something said, "Is this mead?"

Alexander nodded.

"I'm afraid I am going to have to confiscate this," he said and placed the jug on his table.

"Proceed," he said, taking his seat and marking something in his book.

Alexander figured the man would question Filbert and Florian or more closely examine the contents of their cart, but the moment he confiscated the mead, he became eager to get rid of them.

As Alexander passed over the threshold of his homeland and proceeded forward along the road, his heart quickened. He couldn't be sure if it was dread or excitement that brought about the feeling. In reality, it was a peculiar combination of the two.

22

In Which the Twins Only Kill Two People

Fausta stood in the palace library watching the twins. Acacia was browsing a nearby shelf. Jace was leaning back against a little work table regarding Fausta with an amused grin. The place was empty, aside from the three of them. It wouldn't have mattered if it wasn't. The twins always kept her hidden—invisible and unheard by anyone other than themselves. She was a silent spectator as they tortured her people and wreaked havoc on her nation.

"Do you remember Damara?" Jace asked.

Damara had been one of her handmaidens before Fausta found the twins. She had to dismiss her before the coup because she despised Justin and would never believe a kind word about him. Fausta was sorry to see her go. She was a hard worker and the only one of her handmaidens who was honest with her. While the others only showered her with compliments, Damara would say things like, "What is wrong with your hair! No, no! You cannot enter the court like that!" Then, she would herd Fausta back to her chambers and redo everything.

Fausta felt awful about letting her go. Mostly because of her good work and loyalty, but also because she had a very young son to support. She assured her she would want for nothing but that didn't stop Damara from sobbing and calling Fausta heartless. Fausta warned Damara that her boldness was going to get her into trouble one day. She was afraid that day had come.

"Damara?" Fausta questioned. "She was a handmaiden of mine for a while. Why?"

"Was she a friend?" Jace pressed.

Fausta felt her heart starting to race but she kept her expression blank.

"She was just a servant," Fausta shrugged.

"Do you know that she's in prison?"

Fausta felt a knot in her stomach but tried to act disinterested. She looked over his shoulder and noticed that Acacia had settled on a book. Since it was still chained to the shelf, she gave it a jerk, snapping the chain like thread.

"*Apollodoros's History of Kalathea,*" Acacia read. She flipped it open with one hand and started violently flicking through the pages with the other. Fausta was grateful Alexander wasn't there to see her handling a book that way. Acacia skimmed one page, made an amused little snort and snapped the book shut.

"Oh you got that wrong, Apollodoros," she smiled. Then all at once, flames leapt up from her palm and consumed the text leaving her hands dusted in ash. She brushed them off and continued browsing.

"Aren't you going to ask me why she's in prison?" Jace pressed.

"I don't really care," Fausta lied. "If you put her there, that's where she deserves to be."

Jace's grin broadened. He could see right through her.

"Let me fetch her for you," he replied. "Then, she can tell you the whole story."

Just then, Fausta noticed Damara standing between the two of them. She was glancing around in alarm, trying to gather her bearings. She was a few years younger than Fausta and looked remarkably good for someone who had been in prison. She had put her hair up and washed her face and kept her gown unwrinkled—it shouldn't have surprised Fausta; this was Damara's way.

"My Queen!" Damara exclaimed. "What have these demons done to you?"

Fausta jumped. Damara could see her.

"You look awful!" the handmaiden cried.

Fausta swallowed a sigh. Her appearance was the last thing she was worried about at the moment.

Jace grabbed Damara's shoulder and forced her around to face him. Then he looked at her with a gentle, sorrowful expression.

"Damara, I want you to tell the queen what you've done," Jace insisted. "And then I want you to apologize."

She tried to jerk away from him but couldn't.

"How about I tell her what *you* did first?" Damara snapped. "How you drowned Brother Nathan, and then murdered that other man—"

"Oh Damara, Damara, Damara," Jace sighed. "As I explained. We did not drown him. He chose to jump overboard—"

"You could have saved him!"

"Now Damara—"

"My Queen, one moment I was at home, the next moment I was in the middle of the ocean on a rickety boat crowded with a dozen others. All kinds of people—of every age and occupation all as confused as I was. A few I knew, Brother Nathan for one, most I'd never seen.

Then these two show up, standing on the water beside the boat as if it were solid ground. They tell us if we don't throw someone out we are all going to drown—"

"Wait just a moment!" Jace interrupted. "That is not what we said. All we said was not to worry, that you would figure out what needs to be done. It was that idiot at the bow who decided someone should go overboard."

"I am sure you had no idea anyone was going to suggest that," Fausta remarked.

Jace shrugged. "None, what-so-ever!"

"So then," Damara continued. "An argument broke out about who we should throw out. Most thought it should be this poor old man since he didn't have long for this world anyway. Poor thing was terrified. A few jumped to his defense and a fight broke out and water kept splashing in, and then dear Brother Nathan jumped out…"

"I had to admit I didn't see that coming," Jace said.

"I did," Acacia called. "Remember? I told you beforehand."

"You did not," Jace objected.

"I certainly did! Remember? I said that if we pick someone obsessed with tales of martyrs, they would sacrifice themselves for the others."

"After that," Damara continued, "these two, they just disappeared, leaving us confused and abandoned. We drifted a day and a night before we saw land." Damara's cheeks flushed red and she scowled at Jace. "Then, as we are climbing out onto the sand, frightened and grieving, these two have the audacity to appear and ask us what we learned."

"And what did you learn, Damara?" Jace smiled.

Damara suddenly became very quiet and looked at her feet.

"Tell the queen," Jace encouraged. "You put it so eloquently that day. What did you learn?"

"I told them," Damara hissed, "that they were demons and if they didn't crawl back to Hell I'd send them there myself."

Fausta raised her eyebrows. She knew there was a reason she liked Damara.

"And then everyone else got all riled up and started saying all kinds of hurtful things," Jace continued.

"And you started killing people!" Damara accused.

"Stop exaggerating," Jace reprimanded. "We only killed two people; we had to. They attacked us."

"One moment they were running forward and the next they dropped over on to the sand!" Damara recalled. "Like their souls had just been plucked away!"

"We wouldn't have had to kill them if you hadn't gotten everyone so worked up," Jace scolded "which is why you must be punished."

Acacia gasped. Fausta heard the sound of another chain snapping. The remnant of it clattered against the shelving causing both Damara and Jace to look over their shoulders at her. She held up the book for Jace to see. "Rouvin's *On the Nature of Women*," she pointed out. Then, she incinerated it as she had the first volume. "I swear, every time I think I've destroyed the last copy, another one crops up! These idiots don't even have a printing press yet, how are they doing this?"

Jace rolled his eyes and turned back to Fausta. "Sorry; where was I? Oh yes, punishing Damara. What should we do with her, My Queen?"

Fausta knew that if she asked the twins to be merciful, they would sentence Damara to a slow and miserable death. However, if *she* suggested they put Damara to a slow and miserable death, they would listen. There was no hope for the poor, stupid girl.

But Fausta decided she could at least offer her a small comfort. The corner of her lip turned upward in a subtle smirk. "I don't punish my subjects for speaking the truth."

A smile flickered across Damara's lips.

"You wound me, My Queen," Jace sighed.

"I didn't realize you were so fragile," Fausta sneered.

Jace grinned, which infuriated Fausta. She wished for just once they would get angry. They only ever seemed mildly amused or disinterested.

"Oh Damara, Damara, Damara," Jace sighed. "Even the queen isn't immune to your corruption! Aren't you even a bit remorseful?"

Damara bit her lip and wrung her hands. Then she took a breath and said: "No."

Acacia strolled over with a book tucked under her arm. She was tossing an apple up and down with the opposite hand. She must have created it through magic because apples weren't in season.

"Where is Augustine?" she asked.

Fausta winced. Augustine was Damara's son.

Damara smiled. "Safe, hidden, someplace far from here."

"And your husband?"

"I am a widow."

"Please," Acacia smirked. "There are no Christians here. You don't have to tell us you're a widow."

"I am a widow!" Damara defended.

"She is a widow," Fausta confirmed.

She was not a widow.

However, the lie was so well rehearsed that it caused no physical change in Fausta and the twins could not detect it.

Jace disappeared for a moment. When he reappeared, Damara went white and her jaw dropped in alarm. He was holding a child in his arms. The boy was about eight—stick thin, all arms and legs. He was in a very deep sleep.

"Look at that!" Acacia remarked. "Where was he?"

"Constantinople," Jace shrugged. "It's like she didn't even try!"

He lay the boy down on the table.

Damara knelt before the twins. "I'm sorry. I never should have insulted you, I—"

"I hate humans so, so much," Jace snarled. "There is no sincerity in any of them!"

"Don't be so harsh, Jace," Acacia replied. "I think Damara is ready to make amends. Aren't you, dear?"

"Of course!" she answered, her cheeks wet with tears.

Anything Fausta said would only make the situation worse. She had never felt so helpless.

"Let's go outside for a bit," Acacia answered. And all of a sudden, that's exactly where they were. Out on some rocky hillside. Fausta could see a small village in the distance, but couldn't tell which one it was.

There were a few others standing in that place, all plucked from here and there across the kingdom, all looking confused and frightened. Damara spun around searching.

"Where are they?" she asked. "The queen? My son? Where are they?"

Fausta realized the twins had hidden her again. It seemed the people could see Damara and the twins but couldn't see her. And she couldn't see Augustine anywhere. Perhaps the twins had left him back at the palace.

"That's not important," Acacia explained. "All you need to know is that if you do exactly what we tell you, your son will wake up where we found him. He won't realize he was ever gone. If you refuse, he will assist us with our next lesson in virtue."

"I'll do anything you say," Damara murmured.

All at once, the whole Earth shook so that the trees bowed and whipped as they were thrown asunder. Fausta instinctively fell to her knees and shielded the back of her head with her hands. There was a deafening crack and then the shaking stopped just as suddenly as it had begun. When Fausta looked up, she noticed a massive split in the ground before her forming a pit about ten times as deep as she was tall. Tree roots sprawled outward from the earth around the perimeter, pulled from the ground as it was torn in two.

Acacia offered Damara a coil of rope. Damara was still clinging to a tree she had stumbled into when the shaking began. She took the rope in a trembling hand.

"What do you want me to do with this?" she asked.

"Tie it to…" Acacia scanned the edge of the pit and then pointed to one of the roots that snarled up out of the newly formed cliff face, "that branch."

Damara did so, treading carefully, so she wouldn't disturb the loose soil near the edge of the chasm.

"And now?" Damara pressed.

Jace shot his sister a little smirk. "Climb down and when you reach the bottom, pull the rope until the branch snaps and falls in after you."

Damara glanced over the edge, wide-eyed, unable to stop shaking. "Then what?" she whispered.

Jace shrugged. "I don't know. Most likely, you'll die of thirst in a few days, unless a lion eats you."

"Or the pit floods, or a rock comes loose and crushes you," Acacia added.

Fausta was shaking with fury and grief, trying desperately to think of something she could say or do to save Damara. There was nothing. She had unleashed monsters on her people and was powerless to stop them.

"How do I know you'll keep your promise?" Damara demanded. "How do I know you'll safely return him?"

Acacia put a hand on Damara's shoulder. "You don't. But think of it this way. If you don't do what we ask, we'll take you back to Lysandria and have your head removed. Then your son will help us with one lesson after another until he's unfit to continue."

"As in dead," Jace clarified.

"If you do what we ask, you will still die but your son *might* not."

Tears flooded Damara's cheeks. She looked up at the twins for a moment, fury burning in her eyes, and then without another word, started down the rope.

23

The Woman in the Pit

There was a small village a short distance from the border. As they passed through, Alexander found himself pointing things out to Filbert and Florian, art and architecture. He told them about Kalathean customs and food and holidays. If they ever got tired of hearing it, it didn't show.

But the faces of the people they passed in the streets did not mirror Alexander's happiness. On the contrary, the villagers had a bitter, weary look about them. There weren't many people outside at all and the ones they did see, seemed focused on their destination. They did not stop to speak to each other. They did not give the three strangers a second look.

Alexander wished he could speak to them, but it was too soon. He couldn't risk being recognized just yet. So he left the village with Filbert and Florian and continued toward Lysandria.

For a long time, they passed only hills and wildland spiraling away from the road in all directions. Then, Alexander noticed the remains of a vineyard. Grapes once carefully tended were left to grow wild. Weeds and thorns pulled at the low hanging vines, desperate to overthrow them.

A little farther along, they passed the remains of another field. It was now a scorched flat, decorated with stray weeds and patches of grass. All the farmland they passed was similarly destroyed or neglected.

"Someone has angered the gods," Florian observed, or at least Alexander thought it was Florian. In all their travels, Filbert neglected to shave and now Alexander couldn't tell one from the other.

Just as the twin that was likely Florian finished speaking, the horses stopped. Their hooves danced up and down in place and they started whinnying frantically. Then, the Earth shook.

"Hold on to something," Alexander ordered.

Filbert and Florian were already gripping the cart. "They know we're here!" probably Florian exclaimed.

"Maybe it's our own God trying to smite you," most-likely Filbert suggested. "I am surprised he didn't do it years ago!"

Probably Florian punched him in the shoulder, "Shut up, Filbert!"

So that was definitely Florian. Filbert was holding the reins. Alexander noted this.

"Or it could just be an earthquake," he suggested.

The shaking subsided.

"That's right," Florian said. "That happens here, doesn't it?"

"Once in a while," Alexander replied, "though I haven't felt one like that since I was a boy."

"Kalathea is wonderful!" Florian exclaimed, "first demon-crabs, now earthquakes!"

"But no blizzards!" Alexander smiled.

He jumped down and started stroking the horses, trying to calm them. "I'll walk up front with them a bit," he suggested. "Earthquakes usually come in sets. There might be a couple more."

"Lovely," Filbert grumbled.

They pushed on, with Alexander walking at the front. After a long while, he saw two men coming up the road in the opposite direction. He guessed they were farmers from the boots they wore, their callused hands, and sun-darkened faces. One was about his age and had a mass of unkempt curls. The other was a few years older and looked as if his expression had been frozen in a permanent frown. They weren't carrying water, or a pack, or any of the usual things one would take on a journey. They were both silent, staring sadly at the ground as they approached.

"Hello!" Alexander called.

"What are you doing?" Filbert whispered.

"They aren't going to know me," Alexander replied.

"But—" Filbert stopped himself because now the two travelers were close at hand. The younger responded to Alexander's greeting with a half-hearted wave; the elder didn't respond at all.

"That was a nasty quake we had earlier, are you alright?"

"That was no earthquake," sighed the younger. "That was the gods hurling a blasphemer into the depths of the Earth."

Alexander raised an eyebrow. "Is that so?"

The younger nodded sadly. "Tore the Earth in half like paper and forced the poor girl down."

"Forced her down?" Alexander questioned. "I thought you said they threw her down?"

"They did!" interjected the elder. "They forced her to climb down!"

"Wait, they made her climb down into a pit?"

"That's what I said," answered the younger. "Forced her to climb into the depths of the Earth."

"Ah, but that's not exactly the same as hurling her into the depths of the Earth," Alexander corrected.

"What does it matter! The outcome will be the same!" the younger pointed out. "Poor girl!"

"*Will* be?" Alexander asked. "She's still alive?"

"She was when we left; poor girl," the younger bemoaned, "poor, poor, girl!"

"Where is she?" Alexander insisted.

"You're not thinking about trying to help her are you?" the older man exclaimed.

"She's been cursed by the gods!" added the younger.

"*Where is she?*" Alexander repeated.

"The gods will smite you!" When the elder said this, he proclaimed it like a vengeful prophet.

"I'll make a deal with you," Alexander proposed. "How about you show me where she is, and then you can watch the gods smite me. I am sure it will be quite the spectacle."

"You're a madman!" the elder returned.

"There's a path a little ways down," the younger said, "across from an old vineyard. Take it up the hill and you'll find her."

The older man glared at him. The younger shrugged. "If he wants to get himself killed, what's it to us?"

"Thank you, sir!" Alexander said snatching a rope from the back of the cart.

"I'll see you at your execution!" the younger replied cheerfully.

"I look forward—" Alexander stopped himself. That wasn't right. "I'll see you then!"

"What did they say?" Florian asked.

"Follow me," Alexander ordered. "I'll explain on the way!"

"Wait, where are you going?" Florian called.

But Alexander was already running away ahead. He heard Florian grumbling swear words and ordering Filbert to stay with the horses. It took him no time at all to catch up to Alexander. He tried to snatch him by the collar, but Alexander dodged and continued running.

"What are you doing?" Florian cried. "What did they say to you?"

Alexander did his best to explain without slowing down.

"Fine! We'll rescue this woman, but you can't just run... off...like that!" Florian panted.

Alexander was beginning to understand Ilona's desire to escape. Filbert and Florian were like overprotective parents.

They had no trouble finding the pit. The trees all around it were tilted or completely overturned, their roots ripped out of the Earth. Alexander and Florian peered over the edge.

The woman was sitting with her back to the rock face, resting her head on her knees. There was a broken tree root at her feet with a length of rope coiled beside it.

"Hello!" Alexander called.

She looked up at him and glared but didn't answer. There was something very familiar about her face. From such a height it was difficult to be sure if he knew her.

"Are you alright?" he asked. It was a stupid question given the circumstances, but he wanted her to talk to him until he could figure out how to help.

"Go away!" she snapped.

He exchanged a confused glance with Florian.

"I am going to get you out of there," he tried. He scanned the walls of the abyss, looking for a way to climb down. The rock face was completely smooth.

"Don't mock me!" she shot back.

"I'm not mocking you," Alexander promised.

The woman regarded him for a long moment.

"You don't know, do you?" she responded. Her tone changed from one of anger, to one of desperation. "You must not help me! Go away! You'll be cursed!"

"So I've been told," Alexander replied. He found a tree branch that looked sturdy enough and started tying the rope around it.

"I've been condemned by those demons who call themselves gods! And unless you also want to become their enemy, I suggest you pretend you never saw me!"

Alexander gave the rope a tug to test the branch.

"I am already an enemy of the gods," he answered and threw the other end down. "Can you climb?"

"I'm not coming out!" she called. "Please go!"

Alexander looked at Florian. "I am going to go down and talk to her."

"What if she recognizes you?" Florian warned.

"Fair point," Alexander replied. "Let's leave her here to die."

"I'll go down," Florian asserted. "I'll tie her up and blindfold her. Then, we can pull her out and convince her it was a good idea later."

Alexander glared at him. "Or, I could convince her to cooperate."

"We can't stay here," Florian argued. "What if the twins are still nearby? Do you know what Ilona will do to me if anything happens to you?"

"Yes," Alexander replied. "And I am so sorry, but we are just going to have to take that chance."

"Why?"

"Because if you attempt to tie her up, and she struggles, and you accidentally hurt her, I'll tell Ilona about it and Heaven help you then!"

"You insufferable little rat!" Florian snapped.

Alexander snatched the rope and slipped over the edge of the pit before Florian could grab him. He descended quickly, almost running backward along the rock face, holding the lead with both hands. When he was safely out of Florian's reach, he slowed a bit.

"What are you doing?" the woman cried. "I told you, I am not leaving."

"I only want to talk," Alexander returned.

"Who are you?" the woman asked.

"Alexander Freeman," he answered. This was the most common name in Kalathea. Alexander had chosen to keep his given name to reduce his chances of slipping up and revealing himself.

"Why do I feel like I know you?" she asked.

"I must have one of those faces," he shrugged. He tried to glance down at her over his shoulder, but immediately stopped himself when he realized how high up he was. "What's your name?" he called instead.

"Damara Hatsi," she answered.

Alexander paused his descent. He knew exactly who she was. His four-year-old self had given her a nick-name: Golden Eyes. This was because she used to wear gold-colored eye makeup which, as a small child, he thought was a natural feature.

Hearing her name took him back to one of his earliest memories. He had woken up from a nightmare, terrified. He remembered trying to sneak into Fausta's quarters and getting caught by Damara. Then, he was surrounded by a pack of handmaidens all fussing over him and pinching his cheeks and playing with his hair, and when Fausta finally appeared, not only did she allow it to continue, she actually encouraged it. Afterward, his younger self made it a point to avoid "Golden Eyes" as much as possible.

Of course, since he'd grown up, he hadn't said much to Damara aside from "good morning" and "thank you" and "have you seen the princess?"

There was something else he remembered about her. She liked to talk. He prayed she wouldn't recognize him.

Finally, when he was a short distance from the bottom, he released the rope. He turned from the wall to face her.

"Justin!" she exclaimed.

Alexander looked confused. "Justin?"

"No," Damara realized, her eyes widening. "Prince Alexander."

Alexander winced. "Who?" he asked innocently.

"You look just like him," Damara observed.

"Just like Prince Alexander? I have been told that."

Damara scowled. "Don't mock me, Your Majesty! I know who you are. I mean you look just like your brother."

There was no denying it. He'd been caught. It was a strange thing. She recognized him so quickly, but if she hadn't told him her name, he never would have recognized her. She looked completely different without makeup (much nicer actually—more human).

Alexander had no idea what to say, or how to explain himself.

"You have some nerve coming back here, after what you did!" she accused.

"I didn't—" Alexander began and sighed. "Can we discuss this later? After we get you out of here?"

"I can't leave," she sniffed. "If I leave, they'll kill my son."

"Oh," Alexander realized. "What if I told you they can't?"

Damara glared and him. "What do you mean by that?"

"Why don't we get you out of here and then I'll explain?"

He noticed her closing a rock in her fist and not a moment too soon. She hurled it at him. He dodged, but it managed to graze his ear.

"Why did you do that?" he exclaimed.

He heard laughing from the top of the pit. He would have shot Florian a scowl if he felt safe taking his eyes off Damara.

"This is a trick isn't it?" Damara snapped. "Those demons sent you here, didn't they? Wanted to see if I'd keep my part of the bargain? Well, I will."

"Why would they send me to test you?" Alexander questioned, rubbing his ear. "You don't trust me; you don't really know me. I doubt you thought much about me since I left."

Damara pondered this for a moment, eyeing him suspiciously. Alexander offered her a hand. She wanted to believe him. He could see it in her eyes. She was also terrified.

She took his hand and he pulled her to her feet. She winced when she put her weight on her ankle.

"Are you hurt?"

She shook her head. "The branch broke before I reached the bottom, but I'm alright."

Alexander made a loop in the rope, and instructed her to sit in it and hold onto the lead with both hands. He hoped she could at least manage that. She did as he said, and then he called up to Florian.

"What ungodly tongue is that?" she demanded.

He suddenly realized he had spoken in Kaltic. Before Alexander could respond, Florian started pulling the rope, drawing Damara up and out of the pit. He hoped she wouldn't be alarmed to find a barbarian waiting for her.

24

Fausta's Handmaidens

Damara was not alarmed at the sight of Florian, but she did take the precaution of picking up a thick tree branch and wielding it like a club. Alexander convinced her to walk back toward the road with them as he explained what he knew about Jace and Acacia. He didn't want to stay there a moment longer than necessary.

Florian noticed Damara limping and said, "You hurt. I carry you."

Alexander winced. When Florian spoke in Greek he sounded… barbaric.

Damara smacked him with the branch. "Don't touch me!"

"We still have a ways to go," Alexander added. "I'll help you if you want."

"Not you either!" she warned. Then, she mumbled, "How is it I get rescued by a murderer and a savage?"

Progress was slow going as Damara struggled along down the hillside. It gave Alexander the opportunity to explain the nature of fairies and his interactions with them.

"I've seen them kill," Damara objected, as she limped through some brambles.

"Were their victims attacking them?" Alexander questioned.

Damara nodded.

"That's the one exception," Alexander answered. "Which is why our only hope of saving ourselves is refusing to play their game. If we refuse to engage them, the game will lose its appeal and I hope they will leave us in peace."

Damara was about to ask another question when she froze in place, listening. Alexander and Florian also listened. It was the sound of footsteps coming up the hill in their direction.

"This way!" Alexander hissed and dove behind a nearby tree. Florian scooped up Damara and followed. He set her down when they were safely out of sight. She scowled at him, and then her attention went back to the path. They were all deeply curious about who was coming in their direction.

Alexander no longer heard anything. He peered out from his hiding place and looked to the left and the right. No one was there.

"It must have been my imagination," came a woman's voice.

Alexander startled and ducked out of sight.

"You've been hearing things since we left!" a second woman hissed.

"Hush!" the first voice said. "They can hear you in Lysandria, for goodness sake!"

Both voices were coming from behind a clump of bushes a little ways down the hill.

"Who is that?" Damara mouthed.

Alexander shrugged.

He saw a face peek out from the brambles. It was a small round face with very bright eyes. Her hair had been tossed up in a bun. "No one!" she chirped and then stood up and ventured back to the path. As she stood a stray lock came free and fell in front of her eyes. She untied her hair and started redoing it.

Alexander recognized her. His four-year-old self had nicknamed her "Angry" because she always looked that way to him. He wasn't sure if she actually was an angry person, or if the thick black eye-liner she wore gave him that impression. It occurred to him that he had no idea what her actual name was. He felt a bit guilty about this. Of course, he couldn't remember the names of half his nobles either.

A second woman emerged. He recognized her also—"Red". Called such because her lips were always scarlet. She wore so much color on them you almost couldn't see her mouth underneath. She was always pursing her lips on one side of her face or the other. His four-year-old self feared Red above all the servants in the household. If she caught him, he'd end up with a kiss mark on his forehead. The greatest frustration of his childhood was that it was almost impossible to get to Fausta without getting caught by one of her handmaidens.

"Do I have dirt on my face?" Red asked.

"Little bit," answered Angry. "Just there."

"Look, your hair is coming undone," Red observed. She undid the bun Angry had just fixed and started redoing it for her.

"Mercy! If Damara sees us like this, she'll wish we'd left her to die!" Angry exclaimed.

Damara gasped. "*Cleo, Zoe*," she whispered. "You think it's really them? Or maybe more trickery?"

Cleo, Zoe, that's right. Alexander had a feeling that Angry was Zoe but he wasn't sure.

"Let's watch a moment more," Alexander replied. He doubted it was trickery. He didn't know why. Perhaps he had been around fairy magic long enough to tell when it was being used. However, there was another reason he wanted to wait.

If his very early memories were correct, these women talked more than all the residents of Lysandria combined. When they were with Fausta in the public halls or the court they, like all servants, remained silent. Then, the moment they entered Fausta's private quarters, they unleashed a torrent of pent-up gossip. If they saw him now, it was likely every Kalathean would know about his return in a matter of hours.

Of course, Alexander hadn't been in Fausta's quarters since he was about five years old. Maybe they had changed.

"Alright, alright, let's go!" Angry ordered, waving Red away from her hair. She looked back at the bush and said, "Come on, Augustine. Let's go get your mother."

Damara was suddenly struggling to peer out from behind the tree.

A little boy popped out from the bushes. His large brown eyes darted around as if some creature was going to jump out and devour him.

"Augustine!" Damara cried and the handmaidens spun toward the grove. Alexander winced. By the time he thought of running, it was too late. The little boy charged after Damara's voice. He burst through the tree line, spotted her, and threw his arms around her. She caught him in a tight hug.

Angry and Red followed suit but paused abruptly when they saw Alexander and Florian.

"You!" cried Angry.

"How?" exclaimed Red.

Then before Alexander had time to say anything in reply, Angry snatched a branch and smacked him over the head with it. She attempted another blow, but Florian caught her arm and forced the branch from her hand.

Red also grabbed a stick and attempted to defend Angry, but this time, Alexander was ready and snatched both her wrists.

Angry struggled to break free of Florian so she could deal Alexander another blow.

"I thought I told you to stay away from him!" Angry screamed at Damara.

"How are you alive?" Red exclaimed, looking at Alexander.

"You don't understand—" Damara started, but Angry cut her off.

"How could you do this to us?" Angry continued. "We came all this way to rescue you only to find you running off with Prince Justin again!"

Red suddenly stopped struggling, realization dawning in her eyes as she looked into Alexander's face.

"Cleo, wait a moment," she said.

So Cleo was Angry and Zoe was Red. It was starting to come back to Alexander now.

"We told you to keep away from him!" Cleo shouted at Damara. "Did you listen, no! 'Those eyes' you said. 'Those sweet, sweet, words,' you sa—"

"CLEO!" Damara yelled.

Cleo stopped struggling.

"Cleo," Damara continued. "This is—"

"Prince Alexander," Zoe answered.

Alexander carefully released Zoe's wrists, and prepared to dodge another blow.

"What?" Cleo cried. "But isn't, but—Prince Alexander is dead."

"Justin is dead, miss," Alexander answered. "I am very much alive."

Cleo turned her head to look at Alexander. "Heavens! You look just like your brother."

Alexander looked at Florian and said in Kaltic, *"Let her go."*

"Have you lost your min—" Florian started.

At the sound of him speaking in Kaltic, Zoe shrieked and smacked him with a branch. He jerked, releasing Cleo. The two handmaidens then scurried to either side of Damara and stood like sentries, clubs in hand, looking suspiciously between Alexander and Florian.

"Even the women in Kalathea are dangerous," Florian grumbled, rubbing his cheek.

"Extremely," Alexander answered, smirking at Florian's misfortune. *"But we both know that Kaltic women are more dangerous."*

"Fair," Florian answered.

"What are you saying?" Zoe demanded.

Florian glared at her. "You bad woman! No..." He paused as he tried to remember the Greek word. He gave up and started smacking his palm.

"You've earned his respect," Alexander answered. "And mine also. Coming here to rescue Damara took courage."

"Where did you find Augustine?" Damara asked.

"I was—" The boy started but Cleo cut him off.

"Zoe and I were in the marketplace—"

"Yes in Elythu," Zoe added.

"You know, because with the queen missing, we don't really have much to do—"

"Because that goddess is always perfect," Cleo grumbled.

"I know!" Zoe agreed. "Without even trying! Those lips! That hair!"

"I hate her," Cleo added.

"So we were shopping for... wait, what was it again?" Zoe asked.

The two went back and forth for several minutes debating what it was they were there to buy. Damara also joined the conversation, suggesting possibilities.

Alexander shot Augustine a sympathetic look.

"What are they saying?" Florian asked.

Alexander held up a finger signaling Florian to wait.

"Anyway," Zoe said. "Augustine appeared right in the middle of the forum."

"Poor thing was so frightened!" Cleo added.

"No, I wasn't," Augustine tried.

"And we were confused because we thought he was in Constantinople," Cleo added.

"And then the gods appeared and told everyone that he was cursed, and anyone who did anything to help him would die," Zoe continued.

"But we couldn't leave him there," Cleo added. "And when we heard about Damara, we couldn't leave her either."

Then, Damara started crying and hugging them and telling them how wonderful they were. And then, Cleo and Zoe hovered around her and all three women started talking at the same time so that Alexander had no idea how each was hearing what the others were saying.

While they were cooing, Alexander relayed the story to Florian.

"They talk a lot," Florian observed.

Hearing that from Florian was deeply amusing because whenever he was with his knights they spoke in a similarly nonsensical manner. (Though in the case of Florian's friends, the conversations usually ended with someone getting punched in the face and then thrown through a table.)

Zoe suddenly gasped and spun around glaring at Alexander.

"You're right! I bet these two were sent to kill us!"

"No, no, no," Damara objected. "I don't think so, I—"

"Do you know what Prince Alexander did before he left?" Zoe exclaimed.

"Yes! And Justin deserved it!" Damara replied.

"I'm not talking about that, I am talking about—" Zoe corrected.

Cleo interrupted. "Justin wasn't that bad. I mean, he wasn't good either, certainly not someone to fall in—"

"Ladies," Alexander interjected. He didn't raise his voice but at once everyone went silent and gave him their attention. "Listen to my story. Maybe it will make sense of things."

He recalled the events that lead to the unleashing of the fairies speaking as little of Fausta as possible. He told them it was the twins who conspired to murder Justin but left out the specifics. These women loved their queen, and would be less inclined to believe him if he spoke poorly of her. (Although it seemed the murder of Justin would only make Damara admire Fausta more.) He told them everything about the fairies he'd encountered on his journey and about all the things these creatures could and could not do.

"I knew it!" Cleo exclaimed. "I knew that woman wasn't a goddess!"

"We'll tell everyone!" Zoe added.

"Please do," Alexander answered. "But carefully. They could have a human kill you if they wanted. Most people aren't as brave as you and may not be inclined to believe you." He paused then added, "Please don't mention seeing me to anyone."

They promised they would not and Alexander felt certain they would try their best.

"We need to find a place for you all to hide," Alexander continued.

"Many Kalts here," Florian said. "Give women to Kalts."

"You'd like that, wouldn't you?" Damara cried. "You disgusting brute!"

Then, all the women started hurling vile insults at Florian. He looked confused.

"What Florian means is that he has men stationed in every village from here to Lysandria. They will hide and protect you if we ask them."

The women mumbled to each other, occasionally shooting Florian suspicious looks as they weighed their options. Finally, Damara turned from her companions and said, "Alright, but you need to give us your knives."

Alexander took his knife from his belt and gave it to Cleo. Damara held out her hand to Florian expectantly. He reluctantly surrendered his weapon.

25

Florian the Philosopher

Alexander wished he could keep Damara off the road, but with her injured ankle, she had to ride in the cart. For whatever reason, Cleo and Zoe were unwilling to leave their friend in the care of a fugitive and a barbarian, and so they insisted on riding in the cart with her. Alexander and Florian worked to rearrange the contents so there would be room for Damara to duck out of sight if anyone came by.

Augustine wanted to sit in the front so he was placed between Alexander and Filbert. Florian was forced into the back with the women. As they pushed onward, the handmaidens spoke among themselves while Florian complained about the arrangement over his shoulder. Alexander was beginning to wish one of the women would whack him over the head again.

It was nearly dark when they saw the village in the distance. They decided that Filbert should run ahead and explain the situation to the Kalts stationed there. Everyone else would make camp and await his return.

After Filbert left, Alexander found a place flat enough that he could drive the cart off the road. They continued around the base of a hill until they found a spot surrounded by trees and rocky outcrops where they would be well hidden. A brook bubbled a short distance away.

"Augustine, want to help me with the horses?" he asked, when they came to a halt.

The boy leapt down at once and helped Alexander unhitch them. Cleo and Zoe started wandering the area, trying to decide where everyone would sleep, while Florian dug around in the back of the cart for provisions.

"What are their names?" Augustine asked as they led the horses to the brook for a drink. There was a bay stallion and a dappled-grey mare.

"That one is Jurian," Alexander answered, pointing to the stallion. "And that one is Calla."

"Like Lysander's horse?" Augustine observed.

"Exactly," Alexander smiled.

Alexander spoke to the boy a bit more as they watched the horses. He asked how he liked Constantinople and what he was studying. The boy was enthusiastic and intelligent. He was very interested in history, which Alexander appreciated. As they spoke, he heard the others chattering behind him as they worked to set up camp.

Once in a while, Florian would call out to Alexander, asking him for the Greek word for this or that.

"I want to learn Kaltic," Augustine mentioned.

Alexander taught him a few words and phrases like: *hello, good-bye, what's your name,* and *where are you from?* As he was doing so something occurred to him.

"Listen," Alexander said. "Don't ask Filbert and Florian to teach you any words."

"Why?" Augustine asked.

"Just trust me."

"Oh! Because they'll teach me swearing," Augustine figured.

Alexander bit his lip. The boy was fast.

"I want to learn swearing! Will you teach me some Kaltic swear words?"

"I don't think your mother would like that," Alexander began.

Just then, he noticed Florian approaching.

"Will you teach me some Kaltic words?" Augustine shouted.

Florian laughed. "Yes! I teach you best Kaltic words! Useful Kaltic words! First, speak to Alexander."

Alexander glared at him and said in Kaltic: *"I'd better not hear that boy say anything indecent."*

"Never!" Florian promised. Alexander knew it was an empty promise, but Florian changed the subject before he could make further objections. *"The women found the swords. They insist on keeping them overnight."*

"Let them," Alexander shrugged.

"What are you talking about?" Florian objected. *"I wasn't going to agree to that! I was hoping you could talk to them; my Greek is somewhat lacking."*

"It's a fair request," Alexander answered.

"They already have our knives! What if they slit our throats while we're sleeping?"

"Why would they do that?" Alexander asked.

"Maybe they're working for the twins."

Alexander thought about that for a brief moment and shook his head.

"Maybe if we show a little trust, they'll return it," he insisted. *"But one of us will have to keep watch regardless. Would you feel better if you took the first shift?"*

When Alexander brought the horses back to camp, the women insisted one of their own keep watch with Florian. Damara volunteered, saying she couldn't sleep anyway.

So Zoe, Cleo, and Augustine lay down on one side of the campsite with a pile of swords and knives in between them. Alexander spread his cloak on the ground on the opposite side of the clearing and lay down, leaving Florian and Damara sitting in the middle, eyeing each other suspiciously. Damara was holding his knife.

As they were a few blankets short, Alexander had given his to Cleo. The ground was hard and he tossed and turned in an attempt to get comfortable. He was vaguely aware of Florian and Damara whispering to each other—probably threats.

He prayed for safety and success and for Ilona's well-being. If everything went according to plan, she was only a few weeks behind him.

He jerked awake when he felt Florian's hand on his shoulder. He thought he had only been asleep a moment, but the darkness was deeper and the moon was higher in the sky.

"Need me to take over?" Alexander asked, sitting up and rubbing his eye with the base of his wrist.

"No, no," Florian replied. "I've a while yet. I need you to translate something for me."

Alexander gave Florian a perplexed look and blinked a few times. "What?"

"I need the word for 'triangle' and 'spiral' and 'universe,'" Florian continued.

Alexander glanced over his shoulder. Damara was still awake, beckoning for Florian to come back and hissing things like, "Leave him alone. It's not important." and "Let him sleep."

"Are you talking philosophy with Damara?" Alexander questioned.

"She complimented my wisdom," Florian explained proudly.

Alexander scowled. Then, rolled back over and closed his eyes.

"Wait, aren't you going to help me?" Florian begged.

"In the morning," Alexander grumbled.

"But we are having such a wonderful conversation."

"You are damn lucky I don't have my knife," Alexander replied, and Florian left him be.

When Alexander woke the second time, he was alarmed to see daylight. He rolled over and saw Florian sitting with his back to a rock and his head drooped onto his chest, sound asleep.

Damara was also where they had left her. Curled up on the ground, clutching Florian's knife in both hands. They had both fallen asleep on watch. Thankfully, the camp was undisturbed.

Alexander climbed the hill a bit, so that he had a good view of the road. While his companions packed things up, he watched for Filbert. It was late morning when he saw him approaching with four other Kalts—knights from Florian's court.

They promised to find a place for Augustine and the three women to go into hiding and send someone to Lysandria to report to the kings. They said goodbye and parted ways. The cart seemed strangely empty as they continued onward.

"Silence at last!" Filbert sighed. He looked over his shoulder at Florian who was sitting in the back. "It's nice, isn't it?"

Florian didn't reply. He was twirling his knife in his hands, while staring absently over the road behind them. He had been holding his weapon since Damara returned it, as if it never occurred to him to put it away.

"*Isn't it?*" Filbert repeated a little louder.

Florian glanced at him, but didn't answer. Instead, he looked toward Alexander and said in Greek: "I need more words. You speak Greek to me."

26

A Familiar Face

"I now know how you survived the siege of 782," Florian commented. He was sitting on the edge of a fountain in one of Lysandria's seven forums. He had made the mistake of pulling a bread crust from his bag and was currently fighting off a mob of pigeons. "You feasted on these damned birds!"

Alexander grinned at Florian's frustration. The three had found an apartment in the heart of the city, and each day, they would sell the goods they had brought in a different marketplace. In doing so, they were able to get a clear picture of the state of affairs.

That day, they were stationed in the largest of these forums—The Forum of St. Valerian. It divided the city proper from the palace walls. Filbert and Florian insisted on calling it a square, even though it was more of a big half circle. They called all marketplaces "squares," which annoyed Alexander. They must have realized it too because they went out of their way to use the word "square" around him as much as possible.

On the northern end stood Kalathea's great cathedral and on the southern end was the entrance to the amphitheater. The "square" was centered by a dangerously pointy obelisk that Lysander the Conqueror had "borrowed" from Egypt over a thousand years ago. And directly parallel that, up a broad flight of stone steps, stood the golden gate that opened onto the palace grounds.

It was a strange thing, experiencing the city through the eyes of a merchant, talking to common folks, seeing the golden gate from the outside. The nobles in the palace were always talking about "the people"—asking what "the people" want and what is best for "the people." Now that Alexander was one of "the people," he was beginning to think that the noble class knew nothing about them at all.

As time passed, Alexander became the talk of the city. For one thing, everyone thought he looked vaguely familiar. His customers would often ask if they had met him before. Alexander would respond with a smile and a shrug and say it was certainly possible, then change the subject.

The other thing that was strange about him was that he wasn't worried about the recent increase in the number of Kaltic immigrants. When it came up in conversation he would say, "Of course, they're coming here. Why would you want to live in Kaltehafen when you could live in Kalathea?"

"I don't like it," one particularly bitter customer complained. "What's to stop them from rising up and seizing power?"

"Oh I doubt the gods would allow that," Alexander replied, innocently.

"It's a wonder the gods haven't purged them from the Earth, the way that they blaspheme."

"It could be that the gods are waiting for the last of them to arrive," Alexander theorized. "So they can smite them all at once, or it could be that what the Kalts say about our gods is true."

What the Kalts said was that the gods were not gods at all, just deceptive beings, using their magic to instill fear in the hearts of their subjects. They went so far as to say that these beings were actually incapable of killing humans or even of hurting them without hurting themselves. Such irreverence was expected of Kalts, but the fact that Alexander entertained their ideas was very strange.

When people pressed him on this, he would say, "Think about it. Have you ever seen them kill anyone themselves?"

Some of the locals said that they had friends who had seen the gods smite people. One swore they killed his distant cousin with a lightning bolt but hadn't actually witnessed the incident himself.

The longer Alexander stayed in the city, the more the people's suspicion of him waned. Those who got to know him found him intelligent and pleasant. He seemed very concerned about how people were faring under the rule of the new gods, and would quietly seek out those who had suffered on their account and offer his assistance.

Over time, his neighbors came to respect him, even if he was unusual. Word of his wisdom and generosity spread. The more the people grew to like him, the more they warned him to stop speaking ill of the gods. They told him that if he continued spouting blasphemies, the gods would retaliate.

To this, Alexander smiled and replied, "I expect nothing less."

After about six weeks, Alexander was standing by his cart in the marketplace. Filbert was speaking to a group of Kalts a few stalls away, glancing in Alexander's direction once in a while as if to ensure he wasn't doing anything dangerous—like going for a walk by himself. Florian had gone back to Elythu. He was going to meet one of the knights he had stationed there with the hope of learning how Damara was faring.

The square was never empty, but the crowd was light that particular morning.

Alexander found himself in the unfortunate position of speaking to his neighbor Linus.

Linus was also a merchant. He sold fabric. He had twenty years of experience doing so and made this known to Alexander every time they happened to set up shop in the same part of town.

That particular day, he took it upon himself to give Alexander advice, telling him he needed to be bolder and "draw people in." Alexander was nodding politely while internally begging God for deliverance.

And deliverance came with the sound of galloping paws. Alexander turned just in time to see a large black dog leaping for him. The next thing he knew, he was lying on his back shielding his face from aggressive licking. The forepaws of the great beast, danced up and down on his chest while the tail whipped violently back and forth.

"Lanzo!" Alexander blurted. Then, he heard another voice cry the same name. He pushed the old dog off so he could stand. When he saw Ilona racing across the square after the dog, mumbling Kaltic swear words under her breath, he struggled to suppress his delight.

"Sorry! Sorry!" she called as she darted through the crowd.

"Are you alright?" Linus exclaimed as Alexander tried to keep the animal from knocking him over again. He had never seen the old dog so alive.

"I'm alright," he promised, and then frowned at Ilona as she looped a rope around Lanzo's neck and tried to pull him away.

"Control that animal, will you?" Alexander grumbled.

Ilona bit her lip. "Sorry! I'm sorry!"

Alexander wanted so badly to ask her how Lanzo managed the trip, but restrained himself. A few passersby stopped to see what was happening. Some asked if Alexander was alright while shooting Ilona dark looks. Alexander assured them he was fine, while Ilona struggled to pull Lanzo away.

Then, something happened, which startled Alexander so much, he jumped backward crashing into his cart.

Lanzo barked.

It was a sound that started in a low growl and grew into a harsh and echoing snap. Alexander had never heard the old dog make any noise other than a sad whimper. Lanzo kept barking as he struggled against Ilona.

"Get that vicious animal out of here before I call the guard," Linus exclaimed.

Alexander heard another voice say they had already called the guard.

Then, the spectators started showering Ilona in a hail of insults and telling her to go back to Kaltehafen. His countrymen had said similar things to Filbert and Florian, but for some reason, seeing them speak to Ilona like that filled him with a burning rage. She had to leave, before he did something stupid and put their whole plan in jeopardy.

Alexander locked eyes with Ilona and mouthed: "*You have no money. You have nothing.*" As he was doing so he found a loose thread on the seam at his shoulder and pulled it so it made a hole.

Ilona furrowed her brow.

"Look what your dog has done!" Alexander exclaimed and the crowd looked from Ilona back to him. "You must pay me for my tunic."

Realization dawned in her eyes.

"No money, sir!" she replied. "Nothing! Nothing!"

Alexander tried not to smile at her purposely broken Greek.

"Then I'll take the dog," he demanded.

Relief washed over her. She mouthed *Thank you*. Alexander noticed Egbert trotting up behind her. She must have broken away from him shortly after Lanzo broke away from her.

The crowd cried out in agreement with Alexander. Ilona furrowed her brow, her eyes moistened.

"Yes, anything, sir! No trouble, sir!" she said.

Ilona gave Alexander the rope and the old dog sat down quietly beside him. His tail thumbed against the cobblestone and his red tongue hung from his mouth.

A guard shoved his way through the ring of spectators and scowled at Ilona and Egbert. Alexander noticed Filbert resting his hand on the hilt of his dagger.

"What's going on here?" the guard demanded.

"Nothing, sir," Alexander replied, "just a minor disagreement. But we've settled things."

"Good," the guard answered, and then looking at Egbert he added, "Take your daughter home before she causes anymore trouble."

"No trouble!" Ilona insisted. "We go!"

As she turned away, she looked over her shoulder at Alexander, amusement glimmered in her eyes. It took all of Alexander's strength not to smile.

"Do I know you?" the guard asked.

Alexander didn't recognize the man.

"Of course, you know him! Everyone knows him!" Linus exclaimed, throwing an unwelcome arm around Alexander's shoulder. "This is Alexander Freeman." Alexander took a step away from Linus. He was one of those touchy people Alexander couldn't stand.

"I know who he looks like!" the guard realized. "He looks just like the young King Alexander."

"People say that all the time," Alexander laughed.

"Who?" Linus asked.

"Remember? Right after Basil and before Fausta, there was that kid?"

"Was there? I don't remember that at all," Linus replied.

"Perhaps you were abroad at the time," Alexander suggested, rubbing Lanzo's head with his free hand.

The guard was scrutinizing Alexander's face.

"Look at me," he ordered.

Alexander did so and the guard brushed his hair aside and stared at his forehead. Alexander let him look just long enough to see that he did not have a scar above his eyebrow and then leaned away from his hand.

"Hmm," the guard shrugged, and then he bid the merchants good-day and continued patrolling.

Fausta stood in the street just outside the palace. The crowd pressed close around her, without seeing her. Jace and Acacia were standing on either side of her, themselves invisible to passersby.

"Notice anything unusual, My Queen?" Acacia asked.

Fausta did notice something unusual. The street was swarming with barbarians, living, and working, and going about their business as if they were native Kalatheans. She had fallen into the habit of playing stupid in the presence of her captors, so in response to Acacia's question, she shrugged.

"You aren't even slightly concerned about all these Kalts?"

She was very concerned. She would have stopped allowing them in long ago, if the twins hadn't imprisoned her.

"Should I be?" she asked.

"The Senate has been begging us to get rid of them for months now," Jace answered.

"I assume that's why you haven't?" Fausta answered dryly.

"Of course!" Acacia answered. "I just love watching those ornery old men squirm."

Every now and then, the twins said something like that—something that made Fausta think they weren't completely evil.

"Also, I am very curious to see what comes of all this," Acacia added.

Fausta furrowed her brow. So the twins weren't responsible for this Kaltic invasion. They were simply allowing it to happen. Fausta's head started hurting as she wondered why. They had complete control over Kalathea. Didn't they want to protect what was theirs? Perhaps they hoped to conquer Kaltehafen also? She wondered why they would want to conquer Kaltehafen of all places.

She didn't know what motivated them. They were almost like heartless little children, destroying things simply for the fun of it. They watched the Kalts with a sparkle in their eyes, like they'd just received a shiny new play thing.

"What should we do with them, sister?" Jace asked.

"I say we leave them be," Acacia smiled. "Supposing they do start fighting with the Kalatheans, who do you think will win?"

"The Kalts, definitely," Jace replied.

"I disagree. The Kalatheans are a proud people with thousands of years of history and culture to preserve. They've been victorious against greater enemies before."

"But we've broken them," Jace answered. "They'd all be gone by now, if we hadn't put a stop to their leaving."

"In all honesty," Acacia answered. "I am getting a bit tired of Kalathea, so I'll make a bet with you."

"Yes?"

"If fighting breaks out, and the Kalts are victorious, I'll let you decide what we do next."

"I want to steal Madhuri's hourglass again," Jace suggested. "So we can go back in time and find out what happened while we were in prison."

Fausta wondered what Madhuri's hourglass was.

"Ugh, why?" Acacia sighed. "We already know what happened!"

"But we didn't SEE it happen," Jace replied.

"Fine," Acacia agreed. "BUT if the Kalatheans are victorious, you have to do whatever I say. No arguments."

"None, what-so-ever!"

Fausta hated both of them. Her kingdom, her people, everything her ancestors fought for and died for were nothing more than game pieces in their hands. Oh, if it were in her power, she'd have their tongues cut out and imprison them in those bottles again. Then, they could spend eternity trapped in their own minds. She smiled slightly, as she imagined the horror of it.

She noticed something that jerked her from her fantasy. A Kalathean merchant, walking through the street with a large black dog trailing after him. He was calling out to someone in Kaltic.

He was older, and he walked with his back straight and his head high, and spoke with a confidence she'd never seen in him. Nonetheless, she was sure it was Alexander. As soon as she realized who it was, she looked down at her feet. Not a moment too soon, she suddenly felt the twins looking at her.

"What did you see?" Acacia demanded.

It would be useless to deny that she saw something. Even when standing at a short distance, they could sense the slightest shift in her. They noticed when her breathing changed or her heartbeat quickened. It was like they could read her mind, though she had managed to conceal enough from them, that she was convinced they couldn't.

She blurted the first name that came to her mind that wasn't Alexander: "Damara."

"Hmm, how did she escape?" Acacia wondered.

"And why did you betray her so easily?" Jace added.

"That's no mystery," Acacia stated. "Fausta has no qualms about treachery."

After seeing Alexander, those words were like a knife in her heart. The twins were both looking toward the place where she had seen him, but to her relief he had disappeared in the crowd.

"Are you going to tell us who you really saw?" Jace pressed.

Fausta shot him a cold glare.

"You know something, Jace?" Acacia interrupted. "It doesn't matter. I am sure we will encounter whoever it was soon enough."

27

The Final Preparations

Alexander was lying on his stomach next to his bed writing a letter.

"Do you know what we need?" he said.

Filbert was sitting with his back to a wall sharpening his dagger. "What's that?"

"A table," Alexander answered.

Filbert glanced around the room. "Where would we put it?"

"We could fit a small one in here." Alexander looked at the words he had written against the rough floor. "I hope Senator Clement can read my handwriting."

He reached up and scratched Lanzo's shoulder. The dog had taken over his bed. It had been a week since they were reunited and the animal had returned to his old ways. During the day, he slept under the cart in the marketplace and at night he slept next to Alexander.

"There's no going back once you contact this Clement fellow," Filbert objected. "I say we wait a little longer."

"Everyday someone comes closer to recognizing me," Alexander insisted. "If we wait, they'll behead me before we even have a chance to denounce the twins."

Filbert pointed the dagger at Alexander threateningly. "No one is beheading you, kid. So stop worrying about that."

Alexander needed to take his place as king so he could denounce the twins on behalf of his people. For that to happen, he needed the Senate to acknowledge his kingship, and for that to happen, he needed to gain their support. This would have been easy except that the Senate hated him and had even before Fausta started poisoning his reputation. Alexander wasn't completely sure why, but he suspected it was because he read everything he signed.

Almost nine months ago, when he was back in his workshop, Alexander explained this dilemma to Ilona.

"Not one of them opposed my execution," he recalled.

Eda, who had been listening quietly, asked, "Was anyone silent?"

One senator had been—Senator Clement. A man who had been in his position as long as anyone could remember. He was a good friend of his father's and not usually shy about sharing his opinion. But the night Alexander was condemned, he hadn't said a word.

"He's your best chance," Eda explained. "Arrange to meet him in a secret place and tell him about the twins."

So Alexander was writing him a note. He had three alternate versions hidden under his bed. He kept second guessing his wording or maybe he was just stalling. He was taking an awful chance contacting the man, but he had no choice.

Suddenly, Alexander heard the sound of heavy footfall approaching the door.

"*That's the landlord,*" Filbert whispered. "*Coming to collect.*"

Alexander tossed a blanket over Lanzo. He was grateful the dog didn't move around much.

They heard the cheerful mumbling of a Kaltic folk song and Florian opened the door.

"I'm back!" he announced.

"So it would seem," Alexander replied, feeling slightly relieved.

"Why are you so happy?" Filbert questioned.

"Because I've been to see our passengers," Florian explained. "Damara is fully healed. She's doing wonderfully."

"Excellent news," Alexander smiled. "What about the others?"

"He only cares about Damara," Filbert accused. "While we are staging a coup, he is off chasing women."

"I thought Damara was married," Alexander mentioned.

"Her husband is dead," Florian grinned.

"From the way you're smiling, I'd say you killed him," Filbert grumbled.

"He died eight years ago!" Florian defended. "Do you know he took six arrows defending Prince Justin. Six!"

Alexander's heart sank. He wondered how many other heroic souls had died in his brother's drunken skirmishes.

"You should have found yourself a wife before the war," Filbert complained.

"I would have, if you hadn't stolen her from me!" Florian retorted.

Then Filbert grabbed Florian's throat and Florian shoved Filbert into the wall and they would have continued fighting if Alexander hadn't spoken up.

"Gentlemen, please! Do you want the neighbors complaining again?"

Lanzo whimpered at the sound of Alexander's voice and Florian released his brother. "What was that?"

Alexander pulled the blanket off Lanzo. Florian's jaw dropped.

"How?"

"I have no idea," Alexander shrugged.

"I told you! Didn't I tell you?" Florian exclaimed. "Not one of my knights is as loyal as Lanzo." He ran across the room and started rubbing the old dog up and down. The tail started thumping, but otherwise the dog didn't move. "What other dog could find me halfway across the world!"

Alexander looked back at his letter, as Florian tried to coax Lanzo over to his bed. He read it over and over again. *He needed more time.* He sighed, folded the letter, and put in with the others.

He lay awake that night, mulling over everything they had yet to do. He had managed to push Lanzo over enough so that he could squeeze in beside him. It was tight, but for some reason he was glad to have the old dog with him.

There was so much to remember, so much could go wrong. He thought of everything Eda told him before she returned to war. Each point was critical, yet complex. Or maybe he was just overthinking it and making it complex. He rubbed his aching forehead.

First, she reminded him that any fairy that kills a human dies instantly. Second, if a fairy causes a human any physical pain, they will feel the pain in equal measure (though it may not be apparent as fairies have a higher tolerance for pain). Last, she warned him sternly, not to use physical force against the twins. If a human attempts to hurt or kill a fairy, the fairy is free to kill without consequence.

Of course, Ilona responded to all Eda's points by asking about every imaginable hypothetical situation, like, "If two fairies stab a human, killing him at the exact same time, which will die?"

Eda's typical response was to roll her eyes and say, "Really? When would that ever happen?"

"Humor me!" Ilona insisted.

"It would be impossible for both blades to kill the victim at the same time. A fraction of a second would be enough to make the difference," Eda theorized.

"Alright, but what if three fairies each put a drop of poison into a glass, the amount each contributed was—"

"I'm done with this conversation," Eda interrupted.

"It could be important!" Ilona pressed.

Eda rolled her eyes: "Since I am not in the business of killing humans, I haven't experimented with the boundaries of this law. I am sure Jace and Acacia could offer more insight."

Sometimes, Alexander wondered if Ilona enjoyed annoying Eda. Of course, Eda was easily annoyed.

Thinking of Ilona brought Alexander back to the present. He missed her terribly.

It was a strange thing. He'd slept alone for nineteen years, but in less than two years of marriage, he'd gotten so accustomed to having her beside him, he couldn't sleep without her. He should have been more comfortable with the bed to himself. Not only did Ilona take all the blankets, she also seemed to become entirely knees and elbows at night, unconsciously jabbing his every vulnerable point.

Alexander glanced over at the twins. They both seemed to be sound asleep. He thought about slipping away by himself for a bit to clear his head. He'd tried to do this before but they always woke up just before he reached the door and insisted on coming with him.

Living with them in close quarters was driving Alexander insane. Then again, he probably went insane long before his journey, around the time he agreed to Ilona's plan.

The poison was working against the gods. It seemed that every day Alexander heard murmurs in the marketplace. Snippets of conversation: "Do you think it's true?" "What would happen if we resisted?" "Why should we submit to their cruelty?"

Though there was much talk about the limits to the twin's power, until someone was brave enough to confront the gods and test the theory, no one was likely to resist them. Alexander had to make his move.

He reached under his bed and found the three letters. He read through each of them over and over trying to determine which he hated least.

28

Annoying the Twins

Alexander woke to the sound of a commotion rising up from the street. He sat up, realizing that he still had one of his letters in his hand. The other two had slipped onto the floor.

He rolled out of bed and collected them, slipping them back into their hiding place before throwing open the window. People were coming out of the surrounding buildings and making their way toward the palace.

"What's happening?" Florian yawned.

"I have no idea," Alexander answered. "But I have an awful feeling about it."

There was a frantic knock on the door.

Alexander turned to answer but Florian grabbed his shoulder.

"Filbert, answer that!" he ordered.

"Answering the door isn't going to kill me," Alexander objected.

But Filbert had already slipped through the curtain and opened it. Alexander couldn't see the door, but he heard the voice of the guard who had recognized him the week prior.

"By order of the gods, the people must all assemble in the Forum of St. Valerian."

The man said nothing else, but rushed away to deliver his message to the next set of residents.

Alexander dressed quickly and was about to exit when Florian caught him by the shoulder a second time. "I'll go out first. Then you, and then Filbert will take up the rear." He looked at his brother.

"Do not let him out of your sight."

"I'll be alright," Alexander promised.

"Of course you will," Filbert growled. "As long as you listen to us and don't do anything stupid."

Lanzo jumped off Alexander's bed and tried to follow them out, but Alexander pushed him back through the door.

"Not this time," he whispered. "No barking."

The three were pushed along in the crowd's current until they were parallel to Lysander's borrowed obelisk. The entire Senate (Alexander counted twice to be sure) was assembled on the marble staircase before the palace gate.

Two beautiful figures stood on the terrace above them. They were dressed in silk and adorned with gold. Alexander knew from a single glimpse that these were Jace and Acacia.

"I'm so glad you've all come!" Acacia announced, as the crowd gathered round. "I think you are going to like what we have to tell you!"

"It's come to our attention," Jace began. "That many of you are beginning to question whether you should follow us."

"It's only natural that you would," Acacia soothed. "Doesn't every child question their parents from time to time?"

Alexander worked his way toward the front of the crowd, ignoring Filbert and Florian's orders for him to stay back. It took some doing as the people were packed in shoulder to shoulder.

"And when children rebel, isn't it necessary for their parents to correct them?" Acacia added.

"Certainly," Jace agreed. "Not to punish, of course, but merely to explain why they need their parent's guidance?"

Alexander stopped behind the first line of spectators. Up close, he recognized many of the senators and didn't want to risk being recognized himself.

"You need us because you are evil," Jace explained. "It's that simple. You fight, you steal, you act selfishly, and you need us gods to…" he smiled venomously, "help you practice virtue."

"We'll show you what we mean," Acacia continued, and then gestured to the senators before her. "You, the people, have decided that these men are the wisest in your kingdom and most worthy of respect."

A few of the spectators snickered.

"You've selected them to govern over you, to represent you. Yet, there is not an honest man among them."

The woman adjacent to Alexander rolled her eyes and mumbled, "I'm shocked."

Those around her stifled their laughter.

"Each of these men," Acacia continued, "has claimed to be superior to the others. Some by their intellect, some by their deeds, and some by being of noble birth."

"Now we demand a sacrifice," Jace smiled. "And we, as gods, demand only the best that humans can offer." He turned to the senators. "Tell me which of you is the greatest? That man will be sacrificed."

The square suddenly became so silent you could hear a scorpion scuttling on the cobblestone. The senators all looked at each other.

"Well, gentlemen?" Acacia pressed. "You always seemed so sure about this before. Why the hesitation?"

That's when Alexander became aware of an opportunity, one he couldn't afford to miss. He heard Filbert and Florian working their way through the crowd behind him. He had only seconds to act, and that was probably a good thing because he didn't want to think too much about what he was going to do.

He broke from the crowd. Filbert and Florian swore as he slipped from their grasp and stood at the base of the stairs.

"I'll make this easy for you," he exclaimed. "I am the greatest by virtue of my birth and I would gladly offer myself as a sacrifice to the gods." The corner of his lip turned up very slightly as he added: "I only ask that they would honor me, by taking my life with their own hands."

"It's true!" cried one of the senators. "This is Prince Alexander, son of our late King Basil. No one can claim to be more worthy than him!"

The entire Senate agreed. All affirming his identity (even the few who hadn't met him), and acknowledging his kingship.

A murmur ran through the people as Alexander's neighbors suddenly realized why he looked familiar.

Meanwhile, Jace and Acacia burst out laughing and didn't stop until they had almost suffocated themselves.

"You know something?" Jace coughed. "I can't remember the last time I was surprised!"

"Delightful? Isn't it?" Acacia replied. "I'd almost forgotten how it felt! You've done us a great service, Your Majesty!"

"Why don't we spare him?" Jace suggested. "He can pick which senator should be sacrificed."

"Excellent suggestion!" Acacia answered. She walked a few steps down. "How about him?"

She pointed to one of the men Alexander remembered as being particularly supportive of his execution.

Alexander furrowed his brow, and stood silently for a moment as if deep in thought. What he was actually doing was reading the crowd. The Kalatheans were captivated by the scene unfolding before them, eager to see how Alexander was going to test their gods. The Kalts were watching the Kalathean guardsmen posted around the square. Most of them were Filbert and Florian's knights, present to protect Alexander and their own kings if trouble arose.

Filbert and Florian were both motioning to Alexander, in an attempt to communicate their displeasure without revealing themselves. Alexander responded to them with a subtle shrug.

Then, he answered the fairies. "By my order, we will not sacrifice anyone to you because you are not gods and we owe you nothing. If you want someone sacrificed, you will have to do it yourselves."

How such a large crowd could go so silent, Alexander didn't know. It was like everyone was holding their breath, waiting to see what the gods would do to him.

"He's much bolder than I remember," Jace smirked. "Last time I saw him, it seemed the only word he knew was 'Fausta.'"

Acacia put her hand on her brother's shoulder and gave him a nostalgic smile. "Oh yes! I remember that! Even when she finally sentenced him, he couldn't quite comprehend her betrayal. He just kept saying her name until they dragged him off."

Alexander felt himself wincing at their words—an anger more pure and more ravenous than any he'd ever felt before was bubbling up inside him. And that was exactly what they wanted. He breathed deeply and silently prayed for the grace to keep calm.

"I know what you are," Alexander stated. "I cannot force you to leave, but I will not serve you either, and I will not allow you to terrorize my people any longer."

"Is that so?" Acacia smiled, then looking up at the crowd, held up her finger: "A moment, please."

All at once, Alexander was standing in a private room in the palace. Jace and Acacia were both lounging on couches looking at him as if he'd just played an excellent practical joke.

"Why are you here?" Jace asked. "I mean why are you really here? Is it because you want vengeance or because you cannot resist the chance to be a king?"

Alexander turned his back to them. He knew they had no interest in dialogue. They were trying to manipulate him. The more he engaged them, the more tools they would have at their disposal.

"No, no," Acacia answered her brother. "You see, taking vengeance or reclaiming his kingdom would be handling his problems. It's Alexander's nature to ignore his problems and hope they go away. Just as he is ignoring us now."

"So why do you think he is here?"

"Hhhhhmmm," Acacia thought, "probably guilted into it by some internal sense of duty."

"How incredibly arrogant!" Jace remarked.

Alexander wondered what he meant by that, but remained silent.

"Isn't it though?" Acacia agreed, "to think that God bestowed some divine mission on him. Alexander would never ignore such a calling, not even if it meant sacrificing everything! I can see why his sister resents him; he's so obnoxiously perfect."

"You've broken him," Jace commented. "Do you hear his little heart racing?"

Were they right? Guilt was part of the reason he'd returned. As he muddled the whole thing over in his head, he was struck with a horrible thought. What if he'd put the lives of Ilona, her brothers, and all those loyal Kalts in danger simply to satisfy his own pride?

He questioned himself, retracing every event, every thought, and every prayer that had led him to where he was now. Second guessing everything until nothing made sense anymore. Who was he to think he could save his people? He had been an awful king the first time; he would be an awful king now. He was worthless, selfish, hopeless, and incompetent. His interference would only make things worse.

Silently, he called to God, saying, *I don't know if I did the right thing. I don't know if my motivations were good or evil. But don't let any harm result from my actions, please. With or without me, save my people from these tormentors!*

As he prayed, two words popped into his mind. The summary of all Eda's warnings, "Don't play."

Alexander turned back to them. "I have nothing to say to you privately. Now, return me to my people or I will walk back on my own."

"Aren't you going to ask—" Jace began.

"No," Alexander snapped.

"...where your sister is?" Jace finished.

Alexander's heart pounded. He desperately wanted to know this. It was bait. He wouldn't bite.

"No," he affirmed and began walking toward the exit.

Suddenly, he found himself stumbling backward, and landed with a splash in a shallow pool of water. When his alarm wore off and he was able to orient himself, he saw that he was sitting in a fountain in the forum where he began. He was on the northern side, in front of the cathedral.

The place was still crowded with people, talking among themselves as they tried to make sense of events.

Alexander couldn't believe it. The twins threw him into a fountain. He had no idea why it made him so angry. After all, he was expecting them to torment him, or find some round-about way of killing him. He never expected something so juvenile. Were they superior beings or spiteful little children?

A woman nearby noticed his stumble, and rushed over to offer him her hand. He couldn't help but smile when he recognized Ilona.

"Are you alright?" she asked.

"Fine, thank you," Alexander replied.

"They didn't get into your head and make you second guess yourself or anything?"

"No," Alexander lied, then immediately felt guilty. Before he could retract his denial, she spoke.

"Your Kaltic assistants are looking for you. They seem very upset. One of them was saying if the gods returned you safely, he is going to kill you himself. You are really irritating the twins, you know."

"Which twins?" Alexander asked.

"Both pairs, actually," she grinned. "Well done!"

Alexander glanced around. The people nearby were starting to notice his reappearance and spreading word to their neighbors.

He gave Ilona's hand a little squeeze and said: "Thank you, miss."

She replied with a warm smile before disappearing into the crowd.

As he stepped out of the fountain, the people circled around him, all talking at once, all asking him and each other, what happened and where he'd been. Then, one of them remembered he was king and knelt before him. All the others followed suit.

As Alexander stood, wet and disheveled, looking over his kneeling subjects, he turned slightly pink and remembered how much he hated being the center of attention. He forgot his humiliation, however, when Jace and Acacia appeared on either side of him. The people fell back, unwilling to stand near the hostile beings.

The gods were looking particularly smug. Acacia was tossing an apple between her hands playfully.

"Alright, Your Majesty," she sighed. "My brother and I discussed it and agreed to surrender your kingdom peacefully if—"

"I don't need you to surrender anything," Alexander asserted. "This kingdom never belonged to you and it isn't yours to return to me."

"But you do want us to leave, don't you?" she asked sweetly.

"Absolutely," Alexander replied.

"We will leave you all in peace, if you prove yourself worthy by passing three trials."

"No," Alexander returned. "Why do you keep acting like this is some kind of negotiation? I can't make you leave, but I am not going to serve you either. Stay or go, it's up to you."

Jace reached out and grabbed Alexander by the sleeve. There it was. That inhuman strength and the powerlessness he felt every time he was confronted with it.

"We've tried to be patient with you, Alexander," he threatened. "But I am afraid your insolence requires a firmer hand."

"Fine, punish me!" Alexander snapped. "Call down fire from Heaven to consume me! Crush me beneath the rubble of these buildings! Send me to my God however you see fit!"

The amusement subsided from the twin's faces. When they made no immediate response, Alexander looked at the sky with an expression of mock concern.

"Is Heaven out of fire?" he jested.

A few of the spectators chuckled. It was only then that Acacia demonstrated her superhuman strength. She crushed the apple she was holding in her fist. It exploded sending pulp flying in all directions. She jumped and looked at the sticky mess in her palm with disgust.

She drew a cloth from the air and used it to wipe her hand clean.

"I'm not omnipotent or anything, but if you can materialize a cloth couldn't you simply dematerialize the pulp?" Alexander observed.

The crowd erupted into laughter.

Jace released Alexander's shoulder with a little shove, sending him tumbling to the ground.

"Arrest him!" Acacia ordered.

Alexander leapt to his feet and looked to see if the guards were obeying. He prayed they wouldn't. The Kalts would rush to his aid, and the last thing he wanted was Kalts and Kalatheans fighting.

He saw some approaching to his dismay. Even if he ordered the Kalts not to interfere, Filbert and Florian wouldn't listen.

"Stop!" one of the senators shouted he pushed his way through the crowd and stood in front of Alexander. "Did we not just acknowledge him as king?"

It was Senator Clement.

He addressed the twins. "If you want to punish him, do it yourselves!"

All the people cried out in agreement. The rest of the Senate, fearing their voters more than any kind of god, also ordered the guards to stand down.

Jace exchanged a look with his sister. She mouthed something to him and he responded with a nod.

Then, all at once, Alexander couldn't draw breath. No one was touching him, he couldn't feel anything in his throat, yet he couldn't inhale.

"Is something wrong, Your Majesty?" Acacia questioned. "You're turning blue."

Alexander looked at Jace. He was standing just behind his sister. His arms were crossed and his brow was furrowed. Alexander could see his own pain reflected in Jace's eyes.

Jace couldn't torment him indefinitely, relief had to be imminent. Alexander crumbled to his knees gasping unsuccessfully. Suddenly, air filled his lungs, never in his life had anything tasted so sweet. His breath left him again, as quickly as it returned.

Jace was now standing before him, releasing a string of vile insults while Acacia stood aside in pained silence. They were switching places, sharing the burden so they could continue tormenting him. Until what? Whichever one killed him would die too.

Alexander crumpled to the ground, and then everything faded and he remembered no more.

29

The Genie Bottle

Alexander woke in a place unlike any he'd ever seen. He sat up, rubbing his horribly sore throat, and drank in the unusual room. It was a large cylinder shape with a dome for a ceiling. Right in the center of the dome, was the circular entrance to a tunnel of some sort. It was wide enough for Alexander to crawl through, but impossible to reach. It was the only way in or out of the room as far as he could see. The walls, floor, and ceiling were all crafted from a single piece of red glass. The perimeter was littered with objects: pots, books, scrolls, and all manner of baubles.

Alexander stood and pressed his face against the wall, trying to see through the glass. He could only make out shapes and shadows.

"So someone's been telling you our secrets," came Acacia's voice.

Alexander spun around to see the twins standing a few paces behind him.

"Did they tell you there are plenty of ways to make someone miserable without killing them?"

"Like trapping them in a bottle for two thousand years," Jace explained cheerily. "Fortunately for you, you won't live that long. Remind me, how long do these things live, sister?"

"Oh… ninety years, maybe, if you take good care of them," Acacia shrugged. "Though he probably wouldn't live half a century on his own. It's amazing how many things can kill humans!"

"Not fairies," Alexander observed.

"Are you sure about that?" Acacia sneered. "Because the Kalatheans just saw us kill you."

"And begged us to forgive them for rebelling," Jace added.

Alexander found this story highly unlikely. He didn't know what the people actually saw, but someone must have noticed how much effort the twins expended strangling him. Even if the people thought he was dead, they must realize that the twins couldn't possibly threaten an entire city full of people unless they had the patience to kill each person individually over a long period.

He thought about making a cynical reply, but he was too exhausted to think of anything clever, and his throat still hurt.

"You know something?" Acacia smiled. "I think this is a more suitable punishment than death. Abandoned in this bottle, tormented by his loneliness, forgotten by his loved ones."

"What loved ones?" Jace asked. "No one loves him, thanks to us!"

Alexander longed for something to shove into his ears. Being alone sounded like paradise after listening to the twins babble on all day.

Acacia snorted. "Now that I think about it, being with his family is probably worse than being separated from them. What a shame we can't bring Justin back to keep him company!"

"What about her?" Jace asked, pointing to a huddled figure leaning against the opposite wall. Alexander could have sworn she wasn't there a minute ago. Her head was bent, and her long dark hair fell around her face, blocking his view. She looked up when Jace motioned to her.

"Alex," she gasped.

Alexander felt a rush of anger at the sight of his sister. His cheeks flushed red; he turned his back to her and stood with his arms crossed glaring at the floor.

"It seems you two have a lot to talk about," Acacia smiled. "Take your time, you have forever."

With that, the twins disappeared. After what did indeed seem like eternity, Fausta spoke in a voice so small he could barely hear her, "I'm glad you're alive."

Alexander ignored her.

"I know you don't want to talk to me," she continued. "So I'll say just one more thing and keep quiet. Everything that happened is my fault and I'm sorry."

She sank to the floor, buried her face in her knees, and for a long time, the room was still. The only sound was an occasional sniffle from Alexander.

He spent so many long hours since his banishment, thinking up things he would say if he saw her again. In that moment, he forgot them all.

When he turned to face her, and opened his mouth to speak, the only word that escaped was, "*Why?*"

"Because it wasn't fair. While Father was sick and Justin was off drinking himself to oblivion, I was keeping this kingdom together. I was—"

"I know why you usurped me," Alexander interrupted. "Why didn't you kill me?"

"What do you mean?" Fausta asked. "Of course, I wouldn't kill you, Alex."

"Why not? You don't love me."

"Of course, I do."

"Do you slander everyone you love?" he snapped, "perhaps it was some sentimental attachment. I was like… some old doll you'd outgrown but couldn't part with."

"That's not true," she scowled.

"That's exactly what it was! You were a little girl and I was a baby without a mother. You rocked me and dressed me and carried me everywhere. Then you grew up and there I was, getting in the way."

She leapt to her feet and stood with her fists clenched, fuming. "You forgot to mention that I defended you, and avenged you, and then managed your kingdom for you. Show a little gratitude."

"Thank you for sentencing me to death and then changing your mind," Alexander replied dryly.

"I was supposed to kill you!" she cried. "How could I leave the kingdom in your hands when you were so, so, incompetent and soft?" She wiped a tear off her cheek. "...And kind and gentle and nothing like what a king should be."

"Goodnight, Fausta," Alexander stated.

He curled up on the floor with his back to her. He doubted he would be able to sleep on the cold glass, but he was tired of talking to her. He was tired in every way.

A lexander made a routine for himself. He started each morning with Dawn Prayer. (He didn't know the actual time or the day so he had to guess which psalms to use.) Then, he would explore his surroundings, looking through all the books and scrolls the fairies discarded. He almost fainted in awe when he found what he believed to be one of Rouvin's original scrolls. Ilona would be so jealous, if he was ever able to tell her about it.

He found a large storage jar and placed the scroll inside. From then on, anytime he found something he thought Ilona would like, he dropped it in the jar. In the days that followed, he added several more scrolls, coins, and jewelry from empires long passed, and a long spiral horn he thought belonged to a unicorn. (It actually came from a narwal.) He would probably never be able to show her the things he collected, but doing it made him feel close to her, so he persisted.

He noticed charcoal drawings scattered on the walls, and started looking for the charcoal. He found a few chard sticks in one of the pots and began to cover the walls and the floor with drawings of his own.

Fausta tried to avoid him, which was difficult given the circumstances. She usually sat quietly in her place, with her face buried in her knees.

He prayed again at nine o'clock (or what he guessed was nine), and every three hours afterward until he went to sleep. Since the Divine Office was usually prayed in a group, he tried to convince Fausta to join him. She agreed, but was out of practice and kept forgetting bits and stumbling over words.

Twice a day, food would materialize in the middle of the room. It consisted of dry bread, and raw vegetables. Sometimes, there was an egg or two. He was never starving, but never fully satisfied either. In a strange way, he found it amusing. The twins couldn't torture him, but they made sure he was always slightly uncomfortable. The room was always just a little too warm, or a little too cold.

He had left so quickly the morning they captured him, that he forgot to put on his cloak. How he wished he had it to spread underneath him. As it was, he slept directly on the cold glass with one arm folded under his head like a pillow. He was dressed in a simple knee-length tunic, with a belt around his waist and sandals on his feet.

Alexander made a mark on the wall every morning, counting the days of his captivity. The more scratches he made, the more he longed for human companionship. Soon, he became so desperate that he set his anger aside and spoke with Fausta for hours. He told her his story, leaving out only a few minor details, like the existence of Ilona. He didn't know if the twins were listening but didn't want to chance it. When he told her about the service he rendered Filbert and Florian, she laughed.

"Father would be furious. He really hated Kalts."

"Did he?" Alexander asked. "I mean… more than any other barbarian people?"

"Oh yes," Fausta replied. "Strange how he could forgive Justin for one drunken outburst after another but couldn't forgive the Kalts for something that happened hundreds of years ago."

"Father loved Justin as much as either of us," Alexander rationalized.

"Really?" Fausta questioned. "Then why'd he look the other way when Justin was abusing you?"

Alexander had no answer and he didn't like to think about it.

"I, for one, will always be grateful to the Kalts," Fausta commented. "For putting Justin in his place." She grinned, and then added. "They are the reason he drinks, you know."

Alexander snorted. Justin had, at one time or another, blamed every living thing in the palace for his addiction. "I wouldn't be this way if Father raised me right!" he would say. To Fausta he would assert, "I wouldn't be like this if you weren't Father's favorite." He was particularly cruel to Alexander, telling him he wouldn't be a drunk if Alexander hadn't killed their mother. It took Fausta ages to convince Alexander he wasn't responsible.

"In all fairness," Alexander smiled. "If Justin told me the Kaltic kings were the reason for his drinking, I might actually believe him."

When they spoke about the past, their family, and all the good and bad that came with it; it was almost like Fausta never betrayed him. She was the same sister he'd always known. But then, he'd think about her betrayal, and it would hurt more deeply than ever, and he'd go lie in his usual place with his back to her.

One evening, as Alexander was lying on the floor trying to sleep, he looked up at the wall and counted fifty-nine marks. With the thought of the sixtieth day, the reality of his imprisonment pierced him. He was never going to see Ilona again.

He rolled over to face the wall so Fausta wouldn't notice the tears on his cheeks. What if the twin's story was true and the people were worshiping them again? That would mean he lost her for nothing. He supposed he would never know what happened to his people, at least not in this life.

30

The Acting Regent

Alexander lay on his side, with a scrap of charcoal in his hand, adding a drawing to the last free bit of wall space. The artwork on the translucent red walls gave them a stained glass look that was at once beautiful and a little eerie.

He suddenly got the keen sense that someone was watching him, someone that wasn't Fausta. He looked over his shoulder and noticed Acacia had materialized in the middle of the room. It was alarming how silent she could be.

"Good morning, little king," she smiled.

He returned her greeting with a cold glare and then stood up and said, "To what do I owe this honor?"

Fausta, who had been sitting trying to comb the tangles out of her hair with her fingers, stood to see what was happening.

"Are you feeling a bit lonely?" Acacia smiled.

Alexander didn't want to give her the satisfaction of an answer so he remained silent.

"Don't pretend you aren't," Acacia continued. "I have seen your tears; I know how terribly you miss your queen."

Alexander felt a knot in his stomach. He looked at Fausta.

"No, no," Acacia corrected. "I said *your* queen."

"What is she talking about, Alex?" Fausta asked.

"I'm not completely heartless," Acacia grinned. "Let's go pay your lovely wife a visit."

At once Alexander was standing in the blinding light of the Kalathean sun, looking up at the walls of Lysandria. As he stood, he realized he was dressed in the white and golden tunica of a Kalathean king. He was wearing a purple cloak that was fastened over his right shoulder with an ornate brooch. He felt clean and neatly groomed. He rubbed his cheek, confirming that the stubble he'd grown in prison was gone. They wanted him to look like a king.

"What is the meaning of this?" he demanded.

But before Acacia could reply, Jace appeared beside his sister.

"I found it!" he called. He was holding Alexander's crown. He placed it on the king's head and stepped back to examine his work.

"How does he look?" Jace asked.

"Perfect!" Acacia replied. "Exactly like a king should!"

"If you can change my entire appearance simply by willing it, why did you have to steal my crown?"

"Authenticity!" Jace chirped.

"Really?" Alexander responded dryly. Fairies did love theatrics.

Jace forced Alexander's hands behind his back and bound them. Then, he looped a rope around his neck and started leading him to the city gate like a dog on a leash.

"What are you doing?" Alexander asked, knowing full well he wasn't going to get an answer. A watchman posted above the gate spotted them approaching. He disappeared and, a moment later, reappeared running down the main road ahead of them.

The city gate was open and the sentries posted around it made no attempt to stop them passing. A few ran in ahead, and started herding people off the street. They didn't need much encouragement, at the sight of the twins they scattered in all directions, disappearing into buildings and alleys.

As Alexander witnessed the Lysandrians' uncanny behavior, he smiled. "So they surrendered, did they?"

The twins were uncharacteristically quiet as they led Alexander all the way down the main road to the golden palace gate. The guards did not open it for them but made no attempt to stop them either. The twins opened it. At least, Alexander assumed it was them; it opened by itself.

He hated how fairies could do magic just by willing it. If they waved a wand or chanted a spell or something, it would give him a warning. But they made no outward sign at all, and the way magic just happened around them was unsettling.

They entered the throne room to see the breathless watchman speaking to Senator Clement. A few of the other senators were present as were, to Alexander's surprise, several Kaltic knights.

"Where is that barbarian queen of yours?" Acacia demanded.

The senators blushed.

"She's not the queen," Clement corrected. "She's—"

"The king's wife? Next of kin? The legal ruler whether you like it or not?" Acacia asked.

Alexander found himself attempting to conceal a smile when the senator grumbled, "Ah, well, when that law was passed, we never imagined a Kalathean king would marry a Kalt. She's the acting regent until we find the king's nearest blood relative or you are good enough to return him to us."

"What do you want?" Ilona demanded as she stormed into the room. When she saw Alexander, the rage left her. Her mouth fell open, her eyes reddened as she blinked back tears.

The sight of her filled him with a strange and overwhelming combination of joy and horror. She was clothed in white and purple silk. Her hair was done up in Kalathean fashion, and a gold crown rested on her head. She was beautiful.

He was sure that her leadership was what kept the Kalatheans from submitting to the twins, but now that they knew who she was, what was to stop them from taking her prisoner also?

She tried to approach him, but found herself unable to move more than a few steps forward.

"We thought you might want to know about the torments your beloved king has suffered at our hands," Jace began.

"I haven't suffered any torments," Alexander corrected.

"And he will continue to suffer until you surrender to us," Jace finished shooting Alexander a glare.

Alexander burst out laughing. "Is that what this is all about? Getting Kalathea back? Beings as powerful as yourselves, you could go anywhere! Do anything! Tormenting us doesn't even amuse you anymore, does it? You just can't accept that you've lost."

Acacia glanced sideways at him. A rage burned in that glimpse, though she spoke with an even matter-of-fact tone when she addressed Ilona.

"Don't you love him?" she asked. "Doesn't the idea of your beloved rotting for eternity in some filthy prison, bother you?"

"Not as much as being subject to you," Ilona returned.

"As prisons go, it's actually quite clean," Alexander shrugged.

Ilona smiled warmly.

Jace looked at his sister. "What bothers her more than anything is that she has the resources of two kingdoms at her disposal, yet she can't do anything to help him."

Fury flashed in Ilona's eyes. Jace had struck a nerve. Her fists were clenched, her face was scarlet, and she was using every drop of willpower to avoid lunging at his throat.

She locked eyes with Alexander and said, "My brothers are searching every corner of the Earth for Brother Joseph. Don't lose hope and don't you dare submit to them."

"Don't worry," Alexander replied. "I fear you far more than these two."

They exchanged a smile. Then looking to the twins, Ilona declared, "This conversation is over." She stormed out.

All at once, Alexander found himself back in his prison, dressed in his simple tunic and sandals. The twins were nowhere to be seen, but Fausta was gaping at him.

"Why are you smiling?" she asked.

"Because we've won," Alexander replied. "Our people are free."

31

Justin Saves the Dynasty

"You've been keeping secrets from me," Fausta accused.

She was watching him pace back and forth across the room. He had enlightened her on the state of Kalathea. Apparently, the people were being governed by this mysterious wife of his. Fausta was desperate to know more about this woman who had, in ways unknown to either of them, saved her people.

"I have?" Alexander replied.

"I thought you told me everything that had happened since you left, but you never once mentioned her. That's no small detail, Alex!"

Her brother shrugged. He was insufferable sometimes.

"Well," Fausta pressed. "What's she like?"

Alexander's face brightened with a warm smile.

"Bold, intelligent, fearless." Fondness and longing were written in his expression. He paused, thinking and as he thought of her, his smile faded slightly. "She loves to laugh, and she has the sharpest wit of anyone I know. She is playful, kind, and relentless in a fight."

Fausta had never known a man to speak of a woman with such tenderness. Marriages among Kalathean nobles were usually arranged for political reasons. Her first husband was a young senator. Her father said he was a good man—cordial, honest, and fair. She had never known such a description of a politician to be accurate and suspected the true reason for the arrangement was because he was very popular with the people.

Alexander, however, seemed hopelessly smitten with this mysterious woman. He must have used an excellent matchmaker. She hoped he paid her well.

"I can't picture it," Fausta smiled. "You married, that is. You're so monkish."

He looked at her with one eyebrow raised and an awkward half smile, trying to figure out how to take the comment.

"You have any children you forgot to tell me about?"

His face fell. "No." He hugged himself with his arms as if cold and then sighed. "I suppose that's a good thing, given the circumstances." He paced back and forth again. "The dynasty dies with the two of us, I'm afraid."

"Oh I wouldn't worry about that," Fausta replied.

Alexander stopped pacing and looked at Fausta. "Do you have a secret child somewhere?"

Fausta rolled her eyes. Sometimes she wondered if she was the only person in her family who ever noticed anything.

"They're Justin's children," she explained.

"Justin doesn't have any children."

Fausta didn't know why, but there was something slightly amusing about the bewilderment in his expression. He was so innocent. She half wondered if the reason he didn't have children was because he had no idea how to make them. Surely their father wasn't *that* negligent.

"On the contrary," she explained. "He has one in Alexandria, two in Jerusalem, and three in Rome, and one who is back in Constantinople." She wrung her hands nervously. "I hope."

Alexander spent several moments in a shocked silence before blurting out: "How do you know about this?"

"Oh, I read his letters," Fausta answered. "And sometimes, I reply for him. Three of his lovers think he's still alive, you know."

Talking about the letters made Fausta think of Damara. That poor, poor, stupid girl… Fausta remembered the day she showed Damara the collection of intercepted letters. Damara had soaked them in her tears, while Fausta looked on hiding her pity behind an expressionless face. That poor, foolish girl… for a brief moment, the image of Damara climbing down into that pit flashed into her mind. She pulled herself back to the present.

Alexander was still staring at her blankly.

"You thought I took over the kingdom without a plan for succession?" Fausta defended. "When I was crowned, I gave Senator Clement a key to a vault. In that vault is a box that contains the key to another vault, which contains a box with a map showing the location of a chest that contains a list of all Justin's children in the order in which I would like them to succeed me. I instructed the good senator to only use the key in the event of my death. So, you see, our dynasty is in no danger at all. Justin was good for something, I suppose."

"Justin just… abandoned them?" Alexander exclaimed.

How was he surprised by this? Sometimes, Fausta wondered if Alexander remembered anything about their brother.

"He's Justin," Fausta pointed out. "But I made sure they were all well cared for." She then grumbled: "I took care of the last child this family abandoned, after all."

He shot her a cold glare. She had struck a nerve, she knew she would. It amazed her how easily he defended their father. Even after his father refused to acknowledge what Justin did.

"For their sake, I hope none of them threaten your position," Alexander retorted.

Fausta winced. She didn't want to talk anymore. She leaned her head against the glass and closed her eyes.

lexander couldn't bring himself to speak to Fausta for two days after that. It amazed him how Fausta took every opportunity to criticize their father. Couldn't she see how much he loved her, how much he loved all of them?

Certainly, he was distracted, and oblivious. Maybe that was by choice. He was always boasting about his children. Alexander remembered an evening where he sat with Fausta and his father, eating dinner. His father told him Justin was away fighting to liberate the Helevinians.

"You mean sacking Helevinia?" Fausta remarked.

He remembered the way his father tensed. His voice became very stern.

"Why would you say something like that?"

"Because it's true," Fausta shrugged.

His father scowled at her. She rolled her eyes and throwing her arms out said, "Everyone knows it's true! Everyone but you, apparently."

She left the table and stormed out. Alexander remembered how for a moment, his father's whole demeanor fell. He rubbed his forehead and then straightened up and smiled at Alexander.

"Don't worry about her. She's just a bit anxious because of the wedding. Your brother is a good man, a hero! You should be very proud."

Alexander knew from personal experience that Justin was not a good man, but he didn't want to hurt his father by saying so. Alexander had responded in his usual way, by staying quiet and hoping eventually his father would figure things out, or that Justin would really change, or that the problem would resolve itself some other way.

In the present, there was only so long he could ignore Fausta. Loneliness soon compelled him to talk to her again. He resumed his previous routine.

A fortnight passed before the twins made their next move.

32

The Tedious Game

Alexander felt the warmth of sunlight, and the touch of a gentle breeze. He had been pacing in his prison, singing to himself when suddenly without warning he was standing outside the walls of Lysandria dressed in his kingly attire, though this time, his wrists were bound with heavy chains, and there was an iron collar around his neck. It made it difficult to move his head around.

"This again?" Alexander questioned when the twins appeared.

"That queen of yours is a bit stubborn," Acacia answered casually.

"A bit?" Alexander retorted.

"In time, she will see reason," Jace added. "She misses you."

"Thank God for that!" Alexander replied. "If she doesn't, then I have once again been usurped."

Acacia responded with a venomous glare but said nothing else. As they led him through the city, the people responded very much as they had the first time all scurrying out of sight in the wake of the twins. He noticed a few peering through windows or peeking around corners as they passed.

Everything else proceeded as it had the first time, with a watchman running ahead to alert the palace of their approach. When he saw Ilona, he smiled. She forced a smile in return, but her eyes were burdened by sadness and anger as she looked between him and his captors.

"It's wonderful to see you again," Alexander greeted.

"And you," she returned.

"Look at you all!" Acacia accused. "What kind of a nation carries on with ordinary duties while their king is held prisoner? You're incompetent!"

Their desperation was depressing. They couldn't control the people, but if they wanted to hold the king prisoner, no mortal could stop them. It was their spiteful way of asserting themselves.

Alexander gave Ilona a sly smile. "I am not their prisoner. They are mine."

"What do you mean?" Ilona asked.

"They are so powerful, they could go anywhere, do anything! Yet, they choose to give me their time. It's as if they walked into my dungeon, chained themselves up, and started complaining about my cruelty."

"That's tragic," Ilona answered, a slight smile touching her lips. It was genuine and warmed Alexander to his core.

The twins looked past Ilona at the handful of senators who were assembled.

"Do you know how much the people love their king?" Jace asked. "Your failure to protect him is leading them to question your competence."

"Do not engage with them," Ilona ordered. "We are here only to honor our king."

The twins kept calling out, taunting and threatening all present. The people ignored them and Ilona only spoke to Alexander. She told him that the kingdom was healing, that people were coming home, and that things were slowly returning to normal.

"Do not surrender," she finished. "And do not lose hope. We will not rest until we've found some way to set you free."

"I won't if you won't," he promised.

"*I love you,*" she replied, and she said it in Kaltic presumably to limit those who could understand. "*I will see you again.*"

Then, she declared the assembly over and left. Everyone present followed suit, ignoring the twins as they hurled vile insults in every direction. Alexander stood in between them, his heart brimming with admiration. The twins were desperate for one person, just one, to acknowledge them, but no one would, and they hated it.

Acacia gripped Alexander's hair and forced his head back so his ear was parallel to her mouth. She was angry, angry enough to hurt herself apparently. He winced.

"So, we cannot kill you," she hissed. "But we can destroy everything you've built. Will you ignore us as your city falls?"

The smugness Alexander felt was suddenly replaced by dread. His heart pounded in his chest. Instantly, he found himself overlooking the Forum of St. Valerian. They had chained him with his back to the obelisk, with his feet resting on the edge of the stone base. The base was about half a man's height, so he was raised enough that he could see over the heads of the few people who were present.

The twins appeared before him, and the few people scattered, leaving the city guards as the only spectators.

"I swear... nothing in this damned city has changed in two thousand years!" Acacia ranted.

"I know!" Jace agreed. "Why do they still have this amphitheater when they don't have gladiator battles anymore?"

"I miss gladiator battles," Acacia sighed. "Ah well."

Alexander suddenly heard a deafening crack, then the whole Earth shook as the ancient building crumpled in on itself.

The twins looked delighted at the horror on Alexander's face.

"Something just occurred to me!" Jace exclaimed. "If they are welcoming barbarians now, they don't really need a wall, do they?"

The twins disappeared. A moment later, a watchman appeared before Alexander, as the man spun around trying to get his bearings, another appeared next to him.

Alexander knew exactly what was happening. They were moving all the guards off the wall. At last, he heard a distant crack, and a rumble that seemed to shake the whole city. Then before he had time to fathom what had happened the twins were back again.

Their eyes sparkled, they shook with elation.

"If a human army chooses to take advantage of this vulnerability, that's their doing, not ours!" Acacia grinned.

Terrified residents started emerging from the buildings around the square, panicked and shaken. The forum was chaos and the twins delighted in every moment.

Alexander, though shaken to his core, needed to remind the people they were safe. He looked at the twins and said, "Kind of you to move my guards to safety."

Jace sneered in response, his rage betraying itself in his eyes. He suddenly looked toward the great cathedral, and Alexander's heart stopped.

It was a colossal structure. At the front Corinthian pillars, each half as thick as Alexander was tall, supported an ornate pediment. Rising above this facade, Alexander could just make out its crowning glory—the dome.

"Remember when this was our temple?" Acacia said.

"I miss those days," Jace sighed. "We leave for a thousand years, and come back to find they've given it to some Jewish carpenter."

"I never really liked it anyway," Acacia shrugged.

They both disappeared. A few more villagers appeared in the street. Alexander could do absolutely nothing, except silently beg God to spare His house.

One of the pillars snapped, buckling inward. The others followed and the pediment sank down after them landing in a cloud of dust.

Alexander heard an awful shriek and suddenly found himself falling forward. His face hit the stone; the chains that bound him were gone. He had no idea why, and didn't take the time to think about it. He leapt up instantly, his heart pounding as he tore toward the cathedral.

As the dust settled, he saw that it was only the facade that had fallen. The nave and everything beyond it was intact. Acacia was racing across the rubble, desperately hurling stones aside.

She was trembling with rage and her cheeks were wet with tears. Alexander froze drinking in the scene. It took him a moment to notice Jace, lying in a crumpled heap beside the ruins.

Alexander raced toward him, halting by his side. Looking at Jace in that moment reminded him of Eda in the smoldering crater back in Erkscrim. A god made mortal—bruised and bloody, lying still with his eyes closed and his breathing faint.

At once, everything made sense. Acacia was looking for some poor human whom Jace had accidentally crushed when he brought down the front of the church.

It must have been Jace's magic that held Alexander captive because when he was hurt, Alexander was set free. He joined Acacia in her search, as desperate to save his wounded subject as Acacia was to save her brother.

He spotted the person in short order. She was around the side of the church, pinned beneath a pile of wreckage. It was a beggar woman. Looking at her, he had no idea how she was still alive. Fortunately, for Jace, she was.

"She's here!" he called.

The words hadn't escaped him when Acacia appeared by his side. The stones crushing the woman dissolved into dust, and at once she opened her eyes and struggled to her feet. Her wounds were completely gone. Fairy magic never ceased to amaze him. She turned and fled, no doubt frightened of Acacia.

Alexander tried to follow her, but he felt a firm hand grip his shoulder.

It was Jace.

He would have looked completely recovered, except there was something in his eyes, Alexander had never seen—fear. He could actually feel the hand gripping his shoulder trembling slightly.

"Thank you, sister," he smiled.

Alexander had never seen so much effort expended on a smile. He looked at Acacia; she was also unnerved and trying desperately to hide it.

The chaos in the square had settled a bit. Everyone was looking at the twins, anticipating their next move, hoping they wouldn't take the rest of the cathedral down.

Alexander looked toward the people and called out, "Now you've all witnessed their weakness first hand!" He looked at his captors and defiantly rebuked them. "If you insist on tearing down the city, you should really be more careful. I wouldn't want you to get hurt."

Jace became oddly calm. The fear and the anger left his expression and he grinned at Alexander as though he'd just thought of a joke.

Acacia looked at him curiously.

"I hate you so, so much," he hissed, keeping his voice low so that only Alexander and Acacia could hear. "And I've just thought of a way to kill you."

Acacia grinned. "Oh!" she asked eagerly. "How?"

"I will tell you in a moment, sister," he continued. "All Alexander needs to know is that it will be slow, and miserable, and very painful. Oh, and every one of his precious citizens will be there to witness it."

Acacia beamed with excitement. Jace tightened his grip on Alexander's tunic and half pulled, half dragged him up on top of the fallen remains of the pediment. Alexander stumbled along after him, trying to keep himself upright as he was jerked over the rubble.

When he'd reached the top, Jace cried out to the spectators, "You've made your choice! You want us to leave? Fine, we'll go! But not until you've been punished for your blasphemy! Your beloved king will be dead by this time tomorrow."

Alexander didn't have time to see how the people responded. In an instant, he was someplace entirely different. It was dark and damp, and cold. He hugged himself, rubbing his arms and realized he was back in his own clothes. After a moment, his eyes adjusted and he recognized the little room. He was back in the prison where he'd spent that awful night five years ago, awaiting his execution.

33

The Game Concluded

How were they going to do it? How could they kill him without killing him? He couldn't close his eyes without picturing a dozen possibilities. Hiring a human assassin was the most obvious option to him. If the twins used magic to keep his guards from protecting him, would that make them culpable even if they themselves didn't deal the death blow?

The bigger question plaguing him was if his death would be vengeance enough to satisfy them. It was clear to him that they were tired of Kalathea. The game lost its appeal when the people stopped playing. Yet, they were too arrogant to lose or call a draw. They had to win before they could leave.

His head throbbed, his heart raced. He paced back and forth across the prison. He wanted to think about anything else. He was almost grateful when he saw the twins standing by the door watching him.

"Is there something I can do for you?" he asked.

"We were going to ask you the same thing," Acacia offered. The rage had left them and they both had the same calm, confident expressions he was so accustomed too. "You seem a bit nervous."

"Do I?" Alexander answered dryly. "I can't imagine why."

"You know, I sort of like you," Jace smiled.

"Just a few hours ago, you said you hated me," Alexander corrected.

"Oh I do!" Jace affirmed. "But I like you also. It's complicated."

"We like hating you," Acacia clarified.

"I think it's a shame we have to kill you," Jace added. "But, well, those insolent subjects of yours need to be punished somehow, so there's really no way around it, I'm afraid."

"The more you talk, the more I look forward to it," Alexander answered.

Acacia ignored his sarcasm. "We aren't completely heartless," she said sweetly. "So we've come to offer you one last request."

"We can give you anything your heart desires," Jace answered.

"I don't see how this could possibly be a trap," Alexander remarked.

"What trap?" Acacia shrugged. "We are already killing you; what are you so afraid of?"

"I won't play."

"Even if we told you we'd let you see that queen of yours?"

Alexander felt a deep ache in his chest. There wasn't anything in the world he wanted more. He turned to face the prison wall, praying he wouldn't make a foolish choice. After a long moment, he turned back to face them.

"Kindly leave my prison," Alexander replied.

"You are so boring," Acacia sighed.

Alexander had never been so glad to hear anything.

"I know," he smirked "Goodnight."

They disappeared. Alexander stooped down and undid his sandals, and then he curled up on the cold floor. He fell asleep feeling a strange combination of terrified and triumphant.

A lexander woke the next morning to a kick in the ribs.

"Good morning, Your Majesty!" Jace declared cheerily. "Are you ready to die?"

"I hope so," Alexander replied, stretching groggily. "We mortals should always be ready to die."

He looked down at himself, and saw that once again, he was wearing his royal garments. Only, now, the fairies had neglected to put anything on his feet.

"Put your shoes on; everyone's waiting," Jace ordered.

Alexander looked up at Jace with one eyebrow raised. Then, Jace pointed to the floor where two pairs of shoes rested side by side. The first was a pair of thick leather riding boots. They were almost knee high and laced all the way up the front. The second pair were formal shoes with a slightly pointed toe. They were the kind of shoes he normally wore in the royal court and the ones that matched his current attire.

Alexander furrowed his brow. He looked at Jace and then back down at the shoes. What kind of game was this?

He sighed. It didn't matter. He wasn't going to play. Instead, he took his sandals from the place he had left them the night before and started putting them on.

"Don't be stupid, Your Majesty," Jace warned.

Alexander ignored him. "What will you do with my sister?" he asked. He wasn't expecting an answer but he did wonder. Surely they didn't want the burden of caring for a mortal as they went off to wreak havoc in some other part of the world.

Jace grinned. "A better question is what will your wife do to her?"

Alexander looked at Jace curiously.

"Poor Ilona! She is such a passionate woman; she'll want to avenge you. And who is more deserving of punishment than Fausta?"

"You," Alexander replied.

"I was only Fausta's humble advisor," Jace grinned.

Alexander rolled his eyes and decided not to press the matter further. So, the twins were going to release Fausta, or at least hand her over to Ilona. Would Ilona punish her? *Could* Ilona punish her? Did the Senate know about Fausta's crimes? He was suddenly struck with a horrifying thought—what if Ilona had

Fausta executed for high treason? The idea of his wife having his sister killed made him sick to his stomach.

Suddenly, Alexander found himself blinking in the morning sunlight. He was standing in a little valley. It must not have been far from the city, for people were crowding the surrounding hillsides. He recognized many of them. He guessed some magic was preventing them from entering the valley itself.

He noticed his sister standing a few paces away. Acacia was gripping her arm, preventing her from approaching. She must have known there was no way to break free from that grasp, but she kept struggling, unable to stifle the anxiety she felt for him.

"Your Majesty?" Jace said, drawing Alexander's attention back to him. "You'll need this."

He was offering Alexander a sword.

Alexander took it and held it up, inspecting it. "I'm guessing this removes your culpability?" he questioned, and then he slowly swung it over Jace's shoulder stopping it just as the blade came to rest against his neck. "Or are you hoping I'll attempt to cut your head off so you can kill me without consequence."

Jace was completely unfazed. He didn't even flinch at the weapon's touch.

"If you choose not to defend yourself, that's nothing to me," he shrugged.

Alexander lowered his weapon. So this was it. They were going to pit him against someone, or something. Whoever or whatever it was, the twins were confident it would defeat him.

Jace glanced backward over his shoulder. In the hillside directly behind him, Alexander noticed a cave. It was partially hidden behind a patch of bushes. It wasn't a vast opening, but certainly large enough to house a bear or a lion or some other flesh eating creature.

Alexander's heart started pounding as the reality of his situation hit him.

"Where is the Kaltic princess?" Jace called.

"Here!" Ilona called appearing atop the hill.

Jace opened his mouth to address her, but Ilona cut him off.

"No."

"You don't even know what I'm going to say!" Jace protested.

"You're about to tell me you'll spare my husband's life if I fall at your feet and beg your forgiveness, and kiss your perfect little toes."

"How is it you know me so well?" Jace exclaimed.

"You're boring and predictable. Stop talking and get on with it," she replied.

Alexander tore his eyes from the cave and looked up at her. He could tell she was exhausted. Her eyes were red and puffy and framed by dark circles. Despite this, she stood up straight with her head high, staring at Jace with a defiance even the fairy couldn't match.

"Ilona!" Alexander called. "Thank you!"

When she met his gaze, her eyes went glassy. She opened her mouth to reply but then closed it and responded with a nod.

Jace gave Alexander's shoulder a squeeze. "I leave you at the mercy of Kalathea's deadliest creature. Good luck!"

He sprinted away and flopped down at the base of one of the hills. His sister followed suit, pulling Fausta along with her. Alexander gripped his blade, locking his eyes on the cave. Why hadn't the creature appeared? Were they holding it back by magic until now? Unconsciously, he took a step back.

What was Kalathea's deadliest creature? He thought of every wild beast that could possibly come charging at him from the darkness.

The crowd was completely still, all holding their breath. Alexander kept moving backward, wanting to put as much distance between himself and the cave as possible. The valley was full of shrubs and brambles that scratched his feet and snagged his clothing.

Then something struck his ankle causing a horrible stinging pain deep in his flesh. He jumped, glancing down to see a rock viper with its fangs buried in his skin. He swept it into the air with his blade sending it soaring away in two pieces. He slowly lifted his hem and stared in shock at the two tiny drops of blood running down his leg.

He noticed movement on the ground a short distance away. The tail of a second viper, a smaller one, was disappearing into the underbrush.

"Watch your step!" Jace called, playfully.

Alexander laughed bitterly at his own foolishness. Kalathea's deadliest creature…. Of course, this was prime territory for vipers and it looked as if he'd stumbled into a nest. He had chosen of his own free will to walk through the brush in the Kalathean countryside in sandals. It was a foolish mistake, one that anyone could have made. He wasn't watching his feet. He was looking at a cave that was probably empty.

"Do you feel like you've won?" he called.

"We absolutely have," Jace sneered. "I offered you protection, didn't I? But you didn't want to play."

"You're very clever," Alexander quipped. He felt a throbbing pain building beneath the wound. He looked around for Ilona. She had made her way down the hill and was standing presumably as close to him as the twins would allow.

Alexander checked the ground again. He wasn't sure why, but a second bite couldn't make things much worse.

"Do you have any idea how easy it would be for us to heal you?" Acacia mentioned.

Alexander ignored her and, swallowing his pain, sprinted toward Ilona.

"Ah good, run around," Jace commented. "It will spread the venom faster."

Alexander was a few paces from Ilona when he found himself stopped by some invisible force. It was like the air tightened around him and wouldn't release him until he ceased struggling against it.

He stood for a moment, waiting to catch his breath. He couldn't. His heart raced, his hands trembled, and that awful burning pain shot up his ankle and touched every part of his body.

He looked up at Ilona and somehow managed to smile. "It's wonderful to see you again."

"Alex," she began, and then paused as she struggled to hold back her tears. One escaped, and then another.

Alexander hugged himself with his arms as if it would stop the shaking. "Ilona," he breathed. "It's worth it."

"I know," she mouthed.

Alexander suddenly felt like his skin was boiling, a surge of pain and dizziness overcame him, and he crumbled to the ground. He was aware of people talking, calling, shouting all around him. He recognized Fausta's voice, she was arguing with the twins but he couldn't make out what they were saying. The pain increased and soon he couldn't comprehend anything else. It was unclear how long he remained in this state, each moment was like an eternity.

"Alex," came Ilona's voice. He felt her hand touch his shoulder. He opened his eyes and looked up at her. She was kneeling on the ground beside him.

"The—they let you?" Alexander managed.

"They're hoping you will convince me to surrender," she whispered. "They're pathetic."

She sat down among the brambles and pulled him up into her arms, so that she was cradling him across her lap. He took a fist full of her cloak and gripped it so hard he almost ripped it from her shoulders.

After a time, he felt a tingling numbness creeping up his leg. The pain began to subside, and his head cleared slightly. There was something he wanted to tell her, something critically important. He was confused; each breath took a conscious effort. He wished his heart would stop racing for a moment; he wished he could breathe deeply and focus—just for a moment more.

It had something to do with what Jace said before he brought him here.

"Spare Fausta," Alexander pleaded.

Ilona looked surprised to hear him speaking. Or maybe she was surprised by what he asked.

"Alex?" she whispered.

"No one is to harm her," Alexander insisted. His head cleared a bit as he lost feeling in his leg entirely. "This is my last command as king. Make sure the Senate and the people know."

"Of course you'd ask that," Ilona sniffed. "Do you have any malice in you? Are you human?"

"Don't misunderstand me," he pressed. "Put her in prison; just don't execute her. I don't trust her and I couldn't stop resenting her if I lived another hundred years. But…" He paused for a moment trying to catch his breath. "But for reasons that are beyond me, I still love her."

Ilona leaned in and kissed his forehead. "Alright," she agreed. "I will tell them for you."

She wiped her eyes with the back of her free hand.

Alexander smiled weakly. He felt tears on his own cheeks. He wasn't afraid to die, but hated to leave her alone. Fausta's betrayal, his banishment, and everything he suffered in between, was worth it because it gave him the chance to know her. He wished he could say something to express the joy he felt being close to her again.

Fausta looked on from a distance, wondering what they were saying to each other. They spoke for a long time, completely lost in each other, smiling and weeping all at once. Finally, Alexander ceased speaking and lay in her arms with his eyes closed and his lips slightly parted as he struggled to breathe. Ilona continued speaking to him even though he couldn't reply.

It was unclear to Fausta how long it took for venom to complete its cruel task. Each moment stretched on endlessly. Even the twins lost patience and took turns leaving and coming back, sometimes stopping to speak to one another about what they were going to do next. Fausta hated them to her very core.

At last, Ilona stopped speaking and held Alexander silently as a fresh wave of tears flooded her cheeks. She kissed his forehead and then laid him on the ground, gently brushing a stray curl away from his face.

Then, she stood and looked at the twins; at once the tenderness left her eyes, replaced at once by a burning fury.

"Are you happy?" she hissed.

"Are you?" Acacia mocked.

"Why the tears? We've returned him to you. Isn't that what you wanted?" Jace sneered. He approached her and tried to brush a droplet from her cheek. She snatched his wrist and held it as if she was going to crush it in her fist. He pulled his hand free with a playful laugh.

Ilona hugged herself with one arm. It looked almost as if she was trying to keep herself from lunging forward and ripping him apart with her bare hands.

Acacia looked at Fausta and smiled sweetly. "And we've given you what you wanted too. Your brothers are both dead, that makes you queen, doesn't it? No one can say we aren't generous."

"Assuming the Senate doesn't have her executed for high treason," Jace pointed out. "Did we ever tell them about that?"

Fausta buried her face in her hands. She had killed him. It didn't matter that she hadn't dealt the death blow. Alexander was dead because of her. She had killed her little brother, Kalathea's greatest king.

Fausta tore away from the twins and ran toward a group of senators that were sitting together on the hillside. She was able to reach them unhampered. Before them and all the people, she confessed her crimes and begged to be treated as a traitor.

The people murmured among themselves while the senators argued about what should be done. The twins watched the chaos with delighted expressions. Then, a single voice rang out from the valley. It was a soft and pleasant voice that somehow overcame the confusion and brought every soul to silence.

"I'm sorry he killed you," it said.

Fausta turned from the senators and looked toward the speaker. He was a bent old monk with a weatherworn face. He had the darkest skin of anyone she'd ever seen and deep brown eyes that gleamed with a joyous sparkle. A viper slithered around his arms and over his callused hands; he looked at the creature with a broad, warm, smile. The snake looked up at him, its red tongue flickering curiously.

The old man stroked the viper on the head. "He was frightened, you know. Just like you were."

At the sight of the old man, the haughtiness left the twins. They stood petrified, making no attempt to hide their terror.

The old monk stooped down and let the reptile slither into the brush. "Go, finish napping, I'll make sure no one else steps on you."

He straightened up and smiled at the twins. "Well done!"

"What are you talking about?" Acacia snapped.

"Getting one human to practice virtue is hard enough, but look what you've done!" He looked around at the people on the hillside. "You've united the Kalts and the Kalatheans!" He looked at Fausta. She wanted to look away but found she couldn't tear her gaze from those gentle eyes. "You've taught the ruthless how to love." He looked at Ilona and then at Alexander. "And you've made the virtuous heroic."

"You're wrong!" Jace protested.

"You know I'm not," the old man smiled. "If making people better bothers you so much, why don't you sulk off and be on your own for a while."

"Don't you have a war to fight?" Acacia accused.

"Of course not," the old monk replied. "I never fight."

The twins both went scarlet with rage. Never had Fausta seen their hatred so plainly, nor their fear. They vanished without a word.

The old monk turned and began walking toward Alexander. Fausta raced down the hill after him, her heart pounding. As the old man passed Ilona, he gave her shoulder a little squeeze. He knelt down beside Alexander's body and placed a hand on his cold forehead.

"Don't think you can get out of ruling so easily, My King."

The color returned to Alexander's cheeks, his chest rose and fell, and he started murmuring, "Neglecting my duty? What are you talking about?" Alexander mumbled something else incoherent than added: "Fine, Father, I'll go back but just for a little while."

Alexander opened his eyes and Ilona burst into tears all over again. He stared into the face of the old man for a moment with a slightly dazed expression. Then, his eyes lighted with recognition and, to Fausta's surprise, he scowled.

"Where the hell have you been?" he demanded.

"I'm sorry, My King," the old man replied. "I was protecting war orphans from—"

"No, stop," Alexander ordered, holding up a hand. "Just once, I want to be angry at you without feeling guilty about it."

Amusement twinkled in the old monk's eyes. "Alright, go ahead. Tell me when you are feeling better."

Alexander scowled a moment longer, and then seemed to give up.

"I can't do it," he sighed.

The old monk helped him to his feet. Alexander was hardly standing a moment when Ilona threw her arms around his neck and hugged him so tightly that Fausta worried she was going to snap him in two. Then, he kissed the barbarian princess in an uncourtly fashion that made Fausta purse her lips with disapproval.

34

Family and Other Complexities

Alexander walked across the white sand of the Kalathean shore. Ilona was there beside him, her hand intertwined with his. It had only been a few days since they were reunited, and they couldn't bear to be apart. Lanzo was bounding in and out of the water like a little puppy, occasionally bringing Alexander bits of driftwood to throw for him.

"I am not convinced that's the same dog," Ilona mentioned.

"He just needed a bit of sunlight to revive him," Alexander smiled.

"I have some ideas about how we can repair the cathedral," she said enthusiastically. "I've spoken with a number of architects; they gave me all sorts of wonderful ideas."

"I think we should try to replicate the original facade," Alexander suggested.

"Oh no, Alex, the new one is going to be so much better!"

"Not too modern, I hope?" he inquired.

"You'll love it!" she promised.

Alexander was about to ask for more details when Ilona changed the subject.

"Did I tell you Florian is engaged?" she said.

"Is he?"

"Yes! Before he left, he swore to Damara he'd marry her when he returned," Ilona went on.

"Does she get a say?" Alexander quipped.

"No more than you did," Ilona returned.

Alexander was happy for them. He hoped that Damara liked sharing quarters with dogs and livestock. He was about to ask when Florian was returning, when he spotted a messenger running toward them across the sand.

"My Queen!" he fell down on one knee before her and after catching his breath said, "Your brother has returned."

Ilona's face brightened. "Which one?" she asked.

The messenger opened his mouth to reply then paused and blushed, "I think it is King Florian."

Ilona took off toward the palace.

"Don't be so hard on yourself," Alexander mentioned to the messenger. "It isn't because they are Kaltic; they DO look exactly the same."

He called Lanzo and started walking after Ilona. The throne room had a set of main doors at one end, where guests and the public usually entered. Here and there around the perimeter, smaller doors opened onto the palace corridors. Alexander stayed back, watching through one of the smaller doorways as Ilona went ahead to meet her brother. He wanted to give her a moment with him before entering. The main gates opened and Florian arrived, followed by a company of noblemen.

Alexander waited to witness the joyous reunion, but Florian's gait was slow and somber. Looking closer, he noticed tears glistening on the king's cheeks.

Ilona was clearly puzzled by this.

"Florian, what's wrong?" she asked.

Without a word, Florian wrapped his arms around her and said, "Ilona, I am so sorry."

"About what?" Ilona asked.

"I've failed you," he confessed.

Alexander emerged into the throne room and sprinted toward the king. "What on Earth has happened?" he asked.

A collective gasp ran through the king's company, and at the sound of Alexander's voice, Florian released his sister and spun toward him in astonishment.

"You!" he exclaimed, before charging forward and hugging Alexander so tight he almost cracked a rib.

When he released him, Alexander fell into a heap and his guards started over to assist him, but Alexander held up his hand. "I'm alright," he insisted. He rubbed his side as he stood. "This is how he shows affection."

"A messenger told me you were dead!" Florian exclaimed.

"Ah, he must have left before Brother Joseph returned," Alexander observed. "It seems we have a lot to talk about."

They welcomed Florian to a private terrace where they offered him something to eat and told him everything that had happened. It took some time for the shock of seeing Alexander alive to wear off, but when it did, they spoke at length about the state of the kingdom and what the Kalatheans could do to thank the Kalts for their assistance.

After a long time, Florian asked if Alexander would dismiss the servants who were attending them, so they could speak privately.

"Did Ilona tell you about my engagement?" Florian asked. He seemed nervous in a highly unFlorian-like way.

"She did. I am very happy for you," Alexander replied.

"Ah good; Damara recently told me something I think you should know about," Florian continued.

Ilona leaned in suddenly very interested.

"Do you know that Augustine is your nephew?" Florian said.

Alexander responded with a warm smile. He always knew that somewhere under Florian's gruff exterior he had a good heart. But to think he wasn't even married yet and already considered Augustine his own son.

"I know," he answered.

"You do?" Florian questioned.

"It was fairly obvious," Ilona added, with a slight eye-roll and a knowing smile.

Florian relaxed slightly. "Ah, good!"

The conversation then moved to other things.

When Filbert returned the following day, he almost murdered the three of them, for in their joy at being reunited, they forgot to send a messenger to inform *him* that Alexander was still alive.

Luckily, their victory put him in a forgiving mood. They spent a week together celebrating before Filbert and Florian decided to return home. Ilona hugged them both and promised she would see them again one day. Then, the three of them cried and hugged some more.

*A*fter everything Alexander had been through, being king didn't seem so difficult. Sometimes, he even liked it. His duties didn't leave him with much leisure time, but when he found some, he would slip away and paint. Ilona would sit with him as he worked, writing letters and reviewing plans. Jace and Acacia had left the city in need of some serious repairs, which Ilona was delighted to oversee.

During these moments, as they worked together quietly, Alexander almost felt like he was back in Kaltehafen—a warm and sunny Kaltehafen, with a view of the ocean.

There was only one thing that still troubled him. He tried to ignore it for over a year, but it was relentless in its nagging. One night, he couldn't sleep, so he rose from his bed and paced the halls pondering his predicament.

A ways down the corridor, he noticed a dark figure standing in a pool of moonlight looking out of one of the windows, his hands clasped behind his back.

As he got closer, he recognized Brother Joseph. The old monk greeted him with a smile.

"Can't sleep?" the monk asked.

Alexander released a defeated sigh.

"Alright; I'll do it," Alexander said.

"Do what?" Brother Joseph replied. "I didn't say anything."

"I know why you're here," Alexander insisted.

"That's awfully presumptuous of you," the monk answered.

"First thing tomorrow," Alexander promised, before turning back toward his room.

"My King," Brother Joseph called after him.

Alexander paused and looked back over his shoulder at the old monk.

"It's as much for your own good, as it is for hers," he said.

"I know," Alexander answered.

35

Fausta the Historian

Fausta twirled a reed pen in her fingers. She was looking out the window of the tower where she was imprisoned. She was outside the city proper, but she could see the skyline against the brightening horizon. She often found herself looking toward the palace and wondering about her brother's well-being.

It had been a full year since she'd seen him last, and then, he'd made an incredibly foolish decision. He had spared her life (sort of). After she confessed to murder and high treason (among other things), there was no legal way for him to do it. She was technically condemned, but he insisted she help undo some of the damage she had done before her execution.

First, she had to write a detailed account of everything that had happened so that no one would ever repeat the same mistake. Second, she had to make two copies of every manuscript in Kalathea's library. He was horrified to learn about Acacia's book burning and wanted to ensure their texts would be preserved. Given the size of Kalathea's library, these tasks would take around sixty years to complete.

That stupid, stupid, boy. Letting his sentimentality show. She was amazed he hadn't been overthrown already. Then again, he did have an uncanny ability to escape death.

She heard the echo of footsteps, which came to a halt outside the thick wooden door that imprisoned her. It was probably Cleo or Zoe. They came now and then to bring her news from the palace. Damara came a few times too, before she left for Kaltehafen with that barbarian king. (She really did have terrible taste in men.)

But the visitor was neither Cleo nor Zoe. The door opened revealing Alexander.

He stood tall with his head high and his shoulders back. His fingers were laced at his stomach and he was tapping his thumbs together thoughtfully. That was something her father used to do, usually right before reprimanding her.

She hated looking at him. It made her wonder how she could ever justify what she did. But she looked anyway. She had trained her whole life to avoid showing weakness, and to look anywhere else would have betrayed the guilt and humiliation she felt. So she endured it.

"My King," she greeted and it felt incredibly strange calling him that.

He was looking at her the way he had on the day they were imprisoned together. The anger and hurt that burned in those eyes was agonizing. She wanted the Earth to swallow her up.

"To what do I owe this honor?" she asked. Her tone was pleasant and polite.

"Do you know a Norseman by the name of Ivan Eirkson?" he asked.

That was not what she expected. Honestly, she didn't know what she expected, but this certainly wasn't it.

"Yes, is he back again?" Fausta rolled her eyes.

"He seems to think we owe him a substantial sum of money. You wouldn't know anything about this, would you?"

"He shows up every few years. Father was paying him to leave peacefully. Just torch his ships, Alex. It's what I was going to do," Fausta replied.

"I'll take that into consideration," he replied.

Alexander had asked her about a number of similar practicalities in the last year, always by letter or through a messenger. An uncomfortable moment passed in silence. He was regarding her with his brow furrowed. Fausta could tell he was rehearsing whatever he was about to say next in his mind.

She got tired of waiting.

"You came here to ask me about that?" she questioned.

"No, no, just seeing you reminded me that it's something I need to deal with today."

He silently regarded her another minute, and every second Fausta endured that gaze was an eternity.

"Fausta," he started. His voice was so incredibly gentle, and she tensed. That one word was like the prick of a blade that was about to impale her. Why couldn't he just lash out in anger like a normal person?

"It's the strangest thing. I can't feel angry with the twins, at least not deeply. When I think about what they did to me, I feel only pity. How miserable must they be—playing the same games over and over again century after century…? How is it that I feel no resentment toward them, but whenever I look at you I feel it so deeply?"

She wished he would stop talking and just beat her to a bloody pulp.

"You were like a mother to me. I loved you and I still do and as long as that remains true, this anger may never cease to torment me."

Every word was agony.

"But you have confessed and will spend the rest of your life making reparations for your crime. It's done. And so I won't speak of it again," Alexander was going on.

"What are you saying, Alex?" she realized she sounded irritated, but it was only because she was trying desperately to hold back tears.

"I forgive you," he answered.

She responded with a little laugh. (Anything to hide her grief.) Then swung around toward the window and said casually, "You're setting a bad precedent."

A tear escaped her, then another. She was glad he couldn't see her face.

"How so?" Alexander replied.

"I am a traitor, Alexander. Sparing my life was bad enough, but if anyone found out you came here and saw me? They'd perceive you as weak," Fausta replied.

Fausta felt more tears rolling down her cheeks. She managed to keep her voice even and firm.

"I don't want your advice, Fausta," Alexander interrupted. "I came here because I wanted to make sure you knew that I'd forgiven you."

To her horror, she realized her nose was running and that meant she was going to sniffle and betray herself. She wanted him to leave.

Fausta responded without a hint of emotion in her voice. "Leave, Alex."

She heard his footsteps moving away.

"Alex," she called without turning from the window. The footsteps paused. "You aren't thinking of coming back again, are you? Because that would be extremely foolish."

There was a moment of silence and Alexander replied, "Not for a while."

As Alexander left the tower, he felt a deep ache in his heart. He had expected her to react by either joyfully accepting his forgiveness or lashing out in anger and rejecting it completely. She did neither. There wasn't any neat closure, and it was deeply unsatisfying.

All he knew in that moment was that he wanted to be with Ilona. She wasn't feeling well and had been sleeping when he left. He was hoping he wouldn't have to trouble her with any of this in her current state. He thought perhaps he'd slip into their room quietly and see if she was awake.

She was, though still lying in bed. She greeted him with a weary smile.

He knelt down beside her and placed a tender hand on her cheek. "Are you feeling better?" he whispered.

"Much better," Ilona replied. "I was just thinking of getting up."

Alexander shook his head. She kept doing this, and it worried him. She would get extremely nauseous to the point where she couldn't keep anything down, then it would pass and she would insist she was fine. She had been this way for weeks. He wondered if it was something she was eating.

"Don't do that," Alexander urged. "It will only come back again."

"I am fine, really," she insisted. "But I can see that you aren't. What's troubling you?"

"Nothing I want to burden you with," he replied.

"Better you burden me with whatever it is than with the anxiety of not knowing," she answered.

"I went and saw Fausta this morning," he said.

"That explains it," Ilona answered. She stretched and sat up, then patted the spot next to her. Alexander sat beside her on the bed. She didn't look sick, on the contrary, her face was almost radiant. Alexander puzzled over what kind of ailment could come and go as sporadically as this one.

"I take it, it didn't go so well?" she asked.

"I offered my forgiveness."

Ilona rolled her eyes. "Of course you did," she said.

"Are you mocking me?" Alexander asked.

"Only because you're a much better person than I'll ever be," she answered.

"That isn't true," Alexander answered.

"Just continue your story," Ilona returned. "What did she say?"

"She told me I was soft and it could be perceived as weak," Alexander replied.

Ilona raised an eyebrow, "Even from prison, she's telling you what to do?"

"If I condemned her, she'd have lectured me straight to her death," Alexander sighed.

"And probably from beyond the grave," Ilona added. "Death never stopped your father."

Ilona had a way of making Alexander smile even at the oddest moments.

He sighed. "I don't know what I was expecting... maybe some human emotion? Anger? Tears? She was so pragmatic about the whole thing. If she rejected me, that would have been some sort of resolution at least."

"Well, you did what you could do," Ilona replied. "You can't control what she does."

"Is there any truth in what she's saying?" Alexander asked. "Do the people see me as weak?"

She kissed him. "Anyone who perceives you as weak has a very short memory."

She lay back on the bed, rested her hand on her stomach, and smiled up at him playfully. "You're a bit dense sometimes, though."

Alexander furrowed his brow. He had no idea what she was talking about.

It has been almost a thousand years since Alexander died (for the second and final time). Fausta documented everything he did during his reign in great detail. In fact, her histories are part of the reason we know so much about him today. How she kept herself informed from prison is something of a mystery (though scholars suspect a pair of talkative handmaidens had something to do with it).

Kalathea still stands. It's a wonderful place to visit. They have a beach resort there and lots of museums. If you have two Euros and a couple hours to wait in line, you can even go down into the crypt where the Kalathean kings are buried. There are quite a few Basils, Constantines, and Justins, but there is only one Alexander. You'll find him right between Basil the 14th and Constantine the Barbarian.

Stay with your tour guide and do not duck under the barriers. The police are really tired of rescuing lost tourists and may decide to leave you wandering among the skeletons.

When you're finished in Lysandria, take a bus to the Monastery on Cedar Hill. It's hardly changed at all since Alexander's time, except that they've added a gift shop. There is an old monk there, who likes to slip free candies to the tourist children. Many responsible adults have tried to dissuade him to no avail. After all, he was doing that sort of thing long before Alexander was born and will continue doing it long after you're dead.

Acknowledgements

First I would like to thank Pope Clement the 8th who, according to legend, approved the brew of Islam for Christian consumption. If it wasn't for him, I guarantee this book never would have been written.

Second, I would like to thank my four siblings Joseph, Annie, Mary, and Thomas for never trying to kill me. (Actually, I am pretty sure Annie tried to kill me a couple of times, but she was like eight, so I'll let it slide.)

To my writing group, Amelia, Marta, Emily, and Mary, your brutally honest and stream of consciousness notes were so entertaining, I almost published them in the book. (Maybe I should release a special edition with commentary?)

Thank you to everyone who pre-read the book and offered their unfiltered feedback, particularly Tony and Helen who have always supported my creative endeavors.

Thank you, Cecilia Lawrence, for your beautiful cover art. Your creativity and talent blow me away!

No two groups of people are more broadly loathed than in-laws and lawyers. Drew is both my brother-in-law and a lawyer, but by some miracle he turned out okay. Thanks for the proofreading, man.

And, of course, I want to thank my best friend Joe Campbell for his suggestion. Getting married was a good idea.